# ROSELYNN

Edited, formatted, and ebook design by Kristen Corrects, Inc.
Cover art design by BettiBup33 Designs

First edition published 2018
Second edition published 2019

*To Annie, Stevie, and Cole.*
*Watching the three of you reminds me*
*to never let go of the magic.*

# Chapter 1

First off, I didn't believe in ghosts back when I was a little girl. I wasn't crazy enough to hold conversations with dead people no one else saw. Ghosts were the last thing on my mind. My life revolved around hanging around my friends and getting decent grades in school.

Things changed the summer I turned sixteen. I learned to appreciate their otherworldly existence after interacting with a few of them.

Turns out ghosts aren't scary once you understand them. Funny what people accept once they experience things for themselves.

One afternoon Mom sat me down on the couch in the two-bedroom apartment we rented. "Sadie, we need to move. There are no other options." I ran to the room I shared with my little brother Aiden and cried.

I think of all the times I got angry at Mom on the drive across the country to our future home. Who wants to leave friends, school, and their whole life, to end up in the middle of nowhere? I certainly didn't. Compared to California, North Carolina was on the other side of the moon with no way back home.

Falls Creek. A place I'd never visited and barely acknowledged, yet somehow we had a home waiting for us there. Mom said she'd lived there briefly with an aunt and uncle when she was a child, and after being rented out for a while, the home had sat vacant for the past several years. On the rare occasions a maternal grandmother or distant cousin mentioned the name, there was no reason for me to pay attention. Ancient family stories didn't interest me.

No, the only reason we were moving across the country was all thanks to my wonderful dad.

One day, wanting something different, he packed his belongings, informed us he had filed for divorce, and promptly moved out. Once the paperwork got signed finalizing everything, he took off.

Mom now raised two kids by herself.

Who goes six months without telling his own children where he lives or works? You would think that with today's technology, a person would be easy to track down. Turns out, if you don't work a regular job and use cash for everything, it's hard for people to find you. I gave up searching or waiting for a phone call from him. Hopefully he felt guilty, but I doubt it. The whole situation sucked, no matter how many times Mom attempted to convince me otherwise. He didn't call to say hello or send a card acknowledging our birthdays. My few attempts to call him weren't returned.

His selfishness resulted in my mom, brother, and me trapped in the car, headed to a new life far away from friends to parts unknown. Our destination: an old house belonging to Mom's family for over 172 years. With the house rent-free and a front-desk job at a dentist's office waiting for her, Mom hoped this move would make finances easier to manage—"At least until we get back on our feet," she'd promised me. "Then we'll see about returning to California."

Even as she said it, I knew it was a lie.

You probably guessed, I was not a pleasant person on our road trip. I'll be the first to admit to acting bratty all 2,600 miles from California to North Carolina. Stuck in the car with my five-year-old brother, Aiden, whose idea of fun meant singing the same song over and over again, made the miles endless. I hit him twice to shut him up but I got in trouble when Mom yelled at me.

A few times I helped drive, but I tended to fall asleep not long after taking the wheel. Mom poked me awake as the car bumped along the middle of the road, panic on her face. The third time we crossed the yellow stripe, she demanded I be on babysitting duty for Aiden in order to prevent a car crash. Not my fault driving long distances put me to sleep—I didn't do it on purpose—but my eyes refused to stay open.

The side trips to historical sites added little excitement. Mom somehow picked the cheapest and least exciting things. She claimed these types of *attractions* gave us a taste of American history and culture. She called roadside stops *family bonding time.* If we stopped at an amusement park along the way, things could have been fun. Mom claimed such places were too expensive every time I pointed out one as we passed. To me, the journey meant being trapped in the car with no possible escape, as home got farther away.

People talk about road adventures as vacations. Liars.

As you can figure out, our summer journey didn't create fond memories. Not with me still mad at Dad for abandoning us and having to move so far away from everything I ever knew. Saying goodbye to my best friends and leaving my old life behind did nothing to make me cheerful.

Thankfully, I grew up. Turns out the things I thought important at the start of summer weren't a big deal after all, at the end of it. Looking back, I wouldn't change a single thing about my first months in Falls Creek.

Ghosts and all.

# Chapter 2

Finally, we arrived. After endless silent hours in the car, I stared in disgust at the house before me.

All my friends, my old life were replaced with this monstrosity? Life didn't seem fair when I gave up everything to end up here. If only we could move back to our dumpy apartment, I would never complain about it again.

"Mom, seriously?" I didn't attempt to hide the disgust from my voice. I saw no point in faking excitement about our new circumstances. After seeing the house up close I had nothing to be happy about.

With the house built in 1849, I fantasized something grand: a mansion on a large estate, where I could spend a leisurely afternoon relaxing on the porch. Envisioning this got me through many boring miles of empty road.

I hate being wrong.

All the imaginary fantasies in my head didn't prepare me for the actual sight of the house. Mom should have warned me about what we would arrive to. The house was anything opposite magnificent. The term *decrepit* was generous, in my opinion.

Confronted with a falling-down house did nothing to help my hostile disposition. Neither appealing nor grand, one strong shake of an earthquake could cause the house to tumble down all around us. If I knew where my dad lived I'd have taken a picture and sent it to him with a note of thanks for letting us end up here.

Before I complained or expressed shock at the situation we found ourselves in, Mom got out of the car and issued orders. "Sadie, can you help Aiden out of the car?" She struggled to pull two suitcases out of the trunk, leaving me to take care of my little brother.

One glance from her made things clear that it was best to shut up and not speak the words tumbling in my head. Lots of things went through my mind about our new home, none of them good. I couldn't fake being happy about our arrival.

Dark circles under Mom's eyes caused me to experience a minuscule twinge of guilt over my present attitude. It wasn't her fault the situation we found ourselves in, I reminded myself. Our limited financial status left us nowhere else to go. I tried for a moment to be compassionate, knowing Mom left her own life behind too by coming out here. It was hard, though, not to feel angry about my life.

"Yeah, sure," I managed to reply.

Aiden was the only one with any ability to be unfazed by our journey. Unlocked from his car seat and free to run around the car pretending to be a loud airplane taking off, he was not bothered by the state of our new residence. He cared less about the house's horrible condition than playing in the yard.

"Come on Sadie, follow me!" He didn't wait to be chased before taking off.

"No, Aiden. Go into the house. Maybe the inside is better." I hoped my words held some piece of truth. I didn't want my little brother taking off unsupervised in the woods behind the house. We didn't need him lost on top of everything else.

Located an acre from the road and surrounded by a small forest of trees, our new house stood three stories tall. Peeling paint, dirty windows, and broken shutters made for the saddest place I had the misfortune to visit. Brick chimneys on both sides needed a power washing to clean the years of leftover grime. Eight rectangular windows overlooked the neglected front yard we stood in. The paint, peeling after years of limited upkeep, continued to add to the horribleness of the house. The porch worried me it would collapse under the weight of the three of us. To the left of us stood a detached garage with a crack reaching to the roof. We wouldn't be parking the car in there any time soon. Not if we didn't want it buried under the rubble of a collapsed garage.

I didn't know whether to laugh or cry.

On the other hand, the forlorn yard a mess of dried leaves and patches of dead grass gave my overly energetic brother plenty of opportunities to get rid of his boundless energy. Aiden pretended to be a monster destroying villages. After he ignored Mom's instructions to come to the house, I fought the urge to request him to smash our new home with giant monster feet and render it uninhabitable. If we had no house, we had no reason to stay.

His loud animal growls and exaggerated stomping almost made me laugh.

It was too late to turn back to California with nowhere to live, and besides, all our furniture and belongings were on a moving truck somewhere behind us. I contemplated asking Mom to head back anyway. We could meet up with the moving truck and find a new place far from here. This was a better option than walking into the house and having the building fall down on us.

"Come on Aiden, we better get inside and see how bad it is."

"Great, Sadie. That's not helpful," Mom griped.

Taking Aiden's hand and grabbing two backpacks from the car, I followed Mom up the porch steps, resigned to our situation.

"Do we have electricity tonight? It will be dark soon," I asked, struggling to keep all hostility from my voice. The idea of Aiden without his nightlight wasn't pleasant. I can't say I liked the idea of sleeping in a new place in the dark either. Who knew what lurked among the shadows and corners in a place like this.

"The caretaker came this week. There is water and power. Electricity won't be a problem. The house is cleaned. All the beds should be washed and changed. The house has been relatively taken care of," Mom said, standing straight and looking around, "but since this home is being offered to us for free, all the repairs will be on our dime." She looked down at Aiden holding my hand tight. The first smile since lunchtime appeared on her face. "Come on, little man. Everyone inside," she said.

"Me first. Me first." Aiden let go of my hand to rush to the door.

We stopped long enough to let Mom unlock the door before Aiden pushed his way through.

Mom flicked the light switch on and moved out of the way to show an empty entryway long past its prime. Aiden and I had our first inside peek at our new home.

A single light bulb in the ceiling glowed enough to show yellow wallpaper barely hanging to the wall. A wooden floor in need of sanding and a new finish covered the empty entryway.

"See, we made it. And there's power. We'll be fine." Mom's voice sounded hopeful, if her eyes didn't look it.

I added the chore of removing wallpaper to my mental list of things to do. No way would such an ugly color stay on the walls.

To the left of the entryway, a bare room devoid of most furnishings greeted us. Two windows covered in yellow curtains gave us no view of the backyard. A tattered green sofa and a couple of storage boxes piled on top of each other didn't offer a homey feel.

Although the house wasn't decorated enough to make it appealing, at least the front room was clean. No cracks on the walls or water stains on the ceiling indicated the house had been cared for somewhat.

"Mommy. Come here!" The sound of Aiden's voice carried down the hall where we found a small kitchen occupied with a green table and four 1970s-style chairs. Based on the loud humming sound coming from the ancient refrigerator, I counted us lucky our own fridge was coming on the moving truck.

Someone took considerable time to make the inside of the house as presentable as possible. With floors scrubbed clean and things dusted, I wouldn't be playing maid tonight. The room smelled clean, though it looked horribly shabby.

I grabbed Aiden's hand and headed us upstairs. "Come on little man, let's go see what we have." *We might as well get it over with and see everything at once.*

"Be careful! Don't break anything." Mom stayed in the kitchen to put away the food items we brought.

Wooden stairs and a white railing banister led to the second story. At the top of the stairs, a landing with a six-pane window gave us a view of the enclosed backyard. A plank wooden seat attached to two twine ropes hung down one side of a giant tree. Next to it, a small metal bench sat in a shady spot.

The yard, mostly filled with dead leaves and plants, left nothing to enjoy.

Not until I bothered to look beyond the brick wall did the most shocking surprise of the night happen: From my elevated angle at the window, I saw a cluster of old broken headstones surrounded by another brick wall.

I stood in silence. *No way* did I want to live near dead bodies. Not one time in our talks about moving did Mom prepare me for the sight of them.

To be fair, she had not prepared me for anything about our arrival.

The sound of my brother asking questions brought me out of my shock. Not wanting Aiden scared, I yanked him away from the window before he saw.

"Can we play outside?" he asked.

"You'll be able to find lots of bugs for your collection another time. Right now it's getting late. Let's pick out our rooms and get you ready for bed."

By the time I took one last glance outside, Aiden scampered off out of the room. I left behind the unsettling view of gravestones and pushed them out of my mind.

I found my little brother down the hall in another bedroom. The biggest room, with the connecting bathroom, would definitely be Mom's. The wallpaper, replaced with a style closer to this century, gave the room a more updated appearance than the downstairs. She would appreciate an attached bathroom she wouldn't have to share with us anymore. A queen-size mattress centered against the wall next to an old wooden dresser provided the only other furnishings. A single lamp with a cream-colored shade provided minimal light.

"Come on. We need to see the rest of the rooms." I directed him toward the door.

Down the narrow hall, two smaller bedrooms each contained a full-size bed, dresser, and a closet. Both rooms offered a view of the backyard and adjacent cemetery. *Lovely.*

I quickly closed the curtains to block out the darkness, not giving Aiden a chance to peek outside. The sight would scare him too much before bedtime and Mom would have an impossible time getting him to sleep.

"Which room do you want?" I asked while we stood in the last room.

Aiden jumped up on the bed and started to bounce. "I want this one! This one! It's extra bouncy." He waved his arms excitedly. After an unsuccessful attempt to touch the ceiling, he jumped off the mattress with gusto.

"It's yours. Stop jumping. You might break it." I worried the bedframe might fall through the ceiling to the floor below.

Our search uncovered one final flight of stairs leading to the last room of the house. I loved the room at first sight. Awash in white paint, this room too was furnished. A homemade quilt with pale pink and white fabric decorated the single bed. A small closet next to a nightstand offered little storage. I didn't own many clothes anyway, so the lack of a large closet wouldn't pose a problem.

The room was almost perfect for me. The backyard windows offering an unwanted view of the headstones was the only downfall to the scene. I would buy better curtains and keep them closed all the time. The thought of dead bodies would give me nightmares.

On the opposite wall, the view out the front window revealed the driveway and our dusty car with dead bugs splattered on the window. Darkened night skies and trees made the road beyond the driveway hard to identify, although one thing was clear: No neighbors lived nearby. We were on this road all by ourselves.

My small family now lived out in the middle of nowhere next to a cemetery. Of all the things I imagined about my new house, this was not one of them.

If I ignored the contrast to the coming darkness outside, the room itself appeared homey enough once I turned on the light. The idea of a bedroom all to myself provided the only ray of hope. Not only was the room spacious, but a bookshelf also took up one of the side walls. The empty shelves would be full once I unpacked my books.

With my first feeling of happiness, I picked Aiden up from my new bed and gave him a hug.

"All right. You take one of the bedrooms downstairs. The other we can turn into a playroom for you. This room is mine. Let's go find Mom." I headed toward the door.

"Race you!" he challenged, pushing past me to take the lead.

I laughed and watched him take off knowing there was no way to keep up with him.

"I win!" he announced from the first story.

In the kitchen, Mom fed Aiden a cookie by the time I arrived. "Sadie, can you give Aiden a bath now? It's almost his bedtime. I want to finish unpacking a few things." Mom grabbed her suitcase and went upstairs to find her room.

I left Aiden in his new room to play with a few toys as the bath filled up. When I went back to check on it, the water was ice cold. I went in search of Mom.

"Mom, there's no hot water."

She looked up, concern in her eyes. "Shoot. The hot water heater must be bad. People haven't lived here for years, so I can't say I'm surprised. We'll go into town tomorrow to get it replaced. We'll have to make do until then."

I sighed deeply, realizing this meant none of us would be bathing tonight. *Yuck.* Good thing I had showered that morning at the hotel.

I brought something else up that was on my mind. "There are no TVs. Will we have Internet, TV, or radio?" It was important to find out how far civilization was since we only had a graveyard for neighbors.

"Sadie, we aren't in the middle of the desert. The movers come tomorrow. The cable guy will be here in two days. You can survive." Exhausted from the drive, Mom sat next to me on the mattress. "You doing okay?" she asked, without any of the earlier anger in her voice.

I opened my mouth to respond, but Aiden yelled for someone to tuck him in.

Mom chuckled. "To be continued, huh?" She stood. "It's been a busy day. Aiden has the right idea—let's call it a night."

A few minutes later, with a kiss goodnight to Aiden, I left him and Mom reading a book together and headed for my new room. The room, bigger than the one I shared with Aiden at our old apartment, meant no more cramped living on top of each other. I could stay up late without phone conversations waking up my brother. Granted, I needed to meet someone to be able to call them. No point calling my friends in California. They couldn't do anything to help me.

After a quick peek out the front window, I crawled into bed. The outside, quiet due to the lack of neighbors, made the darkness of the room blacker. I distracted myself from the strangeness of my new situation with thoughts of how much work needed to be done on the house.

# Chapter 3

"Sadie, wake up!"

Aiden stood at the foot of my bed. With his curly hair sticking out every which way and thumb stuck in his mouth, my brother appeared little and fragile. Some days he didn't bother to brush his hair. People told him it didn't matter what he did with it. My hair, on the other hand, ended up a mess if I didn't keep it in a ponytail, and I ran the chance of being mistaken for a boy if I cut my hair short.

Seeing him hold his favorite blue stuffed monkey made me grin. His adorableness was contagious, but I pretended to be irritated with his early morning interruption.

"Geez, what time is it? Go downstairs by yourself." He couldn't make breakfast by himself unless I cleaned up the tornado left in his wake but, exhausted, I was willing to make that sacrifice.

"Nope. You need to come." He pulled harder. "I want you to." He refused to leave. The same game we played most mornings, it never got old for him. Aiden believed we should eat breakfast together, even if Mom made it. This was especially true after Dad left. Aiden went through a phase of not wanting to be away from Mom or me. I blamed my dad. It must have been reassuring to have Mom and me there in the morning, so I didn't argue with my brother when he wanted me around.

"Don't ask for cartoons. There's no TV yet."

With Mom's bedroom door closed, Aiden and I walked down to the first floor hand-in-hand. "You can eat cereal and a banana this morning. Let Mommy sleep." The trip exhausted her and I promised myself to be extra helpful today.

His nonsense chatter about superheroes filled the kitchen while I fixed a quick breakfast. His endless talking helped chase away the silence. I was amazed at how quiet a house with no TV or neighbors near could be, and I wanted noise. The only sounds of car and airplane noises come from Aiden.

After I put the used dishes in the sink—no point trying to clean them with cold water—I read a book on the sofa as Aiden played, hoping the movers would arrive soon. Mom came downstairs and joined us. I gave her little time to settle down with a cup of coffee before I asked the question that was on my mind.

"Can I take the car into town when the moving truck gets here?" The idea of being surrounded again by moving boxes didn't appeal to me. Mom yelling directions as belongings were unloaded wouldn't be easy. All the impending chaos reinforced the fact that we were here to stay, and my friends were hundreds of miles away.

Before we left California, Mom had researched driving laws in North Carolina. Here a person could drive at sixteen on a provisional driver's license. Not like driving on a freeway back home with bumper-to-bumper traffic and angry drivers.

The added bonus of no bus service this far out meant limited options to travel. I either borrowed the car or got trapped at home. I didn't do well with no means of escape.

After a brief moment of thought, Mom nodded. "Take the grocery list. Your brother goes too. The house will be easier to organize if I don't worry about Aiden getting in the way or wandering off outside by himself."

I rolled my eyes in frustration. Grocery shopping with a five-year-old who only liked the cookie aisle was never fun. Not eager to take him, but given no choice, I agreed without further protest.

"Buy yourselves some lunch," Mom added, taking money out of her purse. "Come back in a few hours though. I'm not unpacking all the boxes myself. And hey"—she looked at me seriously—"we're a little tight on money right now, so only small purchases, okay?"

I promised to only spend what I thought necessary, I buckled Aiden into his car seat and drove away from the house.

The town of Falls Creek, only ten minutes away by car, made for a quick trip. Driving on a two-lane road, we passed acres of tall trees blocking out any detail of the land behind them. My eyes were on the road, but the few houses

I peeked at were occupied and in good shape. Each house was surrounded by farmland planted with crops I didn't recognize. I didn't know enough about farming to tell what they were. But the land appeared maintained and cared for. We didn't pass a single car, biker, or person until we came to a sign welcoming us.

*Falls Creek, Population 532.*

God, could that be considered a town? Our old apartment complex alone had five hundred people living in it. I slowed the car and almost turned around, not seeing the point of going forward with a place too small for any respectable stores.

Mom moved us to the middle of nowhere.

When Mom told me about the move, she mentioned Falls Creek was built before the Civil War...and upon entering the town, some of the stores looked it. Main Street had three stop lights on a road four blocks long. There weren't enough cars on the road to warrant street lights, but what did I know? Most buildings I passed were made of red bricks and stood one story tall. As I drove up the street, I didn't see well-known names of common department stores—these were all locally owned, mom-and-pop businesses. Instead, with a bakery, one clothing store, a firehouse, and a diner among the few businesses I saw, I realized the shopping options here were pitiful. The only thing that stopped me from crying in frustration was not wanting to upset Aiden with my grievances.

A few side streets showcased housing options for the town's residents. Some looked well cared for, others not so much. Each house's mishmash of colors and styles displayed their owners' unique personalities.

The town surprised me, so different from where I spent most of my childhood where neighborhoods were filled with cookie cutter houses and immaculately cared yards. Here, short wooden and metal fences separated individual houses from their neighbors. With so few residents, crime couldn't have been a problem.

I pulled in to one of the many open spots, and as I shut the car off I reminded Aiden to be on his best behavior. It wouldn't go over well with Mom if we made a bad impression the first visit in town. There might not be many people to notice how my brother and I acted, but I decided it better not to take any chances with the five we saw.

"Be good and I'll buy you a small toy," I promised as I took his hand in mine.

With little need to worry about going broke with so few places to spend my babysitting money, the two of us started our adventure. Our first stop at a bookstore with a storefront window displaying a colorful selection of current and used books piqued my interest.

"Come on! Let's find you a new book for tonight." Reading was one of my favorite hobbies back home when I wasn't hanging out with my friends. I was glad there was at least one good thing about our new town.

A bell chime over the door announced our arrival. For a small store, hundreds of books filled the available space on every shelf.

"Hello. Can I help you?" A young man came into view from the back of the store.

Tall, spiky brown hair, average build, brown eyes. Cute for a guy, if anyone cared to ask me. But since my friends weren't around to discuss the stranger's appearance, I kept my opinion to myself.

"My brother and I are here to look at books." Yes, nothing like sounding intelligent in front of a guy I never met before. I felt the heat rise in my cheeks as I blushed. "Which way to the kids' section?"

Directed to the back of the store, Aiden took off running.

The stranger tagged along beside me as I went after Aiden. "You're the one who moved into Roselynn."

"I'm sorry. What?" I kept an eye on Aiden and tried not to appear rude at the same time.

"The old Meyers' place. Your family moved to Roselynn. All the old places around here are named. I recognize everyone in town, but not you and the little boy. I took a guess. My name is Jackson." He reached out to shake my hand.

To cover my initial embarrassment and shyness, I accepted the handshake. "My name's Sadie. He's my little brother Aiden. We arrived last night. Yeah, I guess we live in Roselynn. Didn't realize it had a name." There was a lot about our new place I didn't know about until my arrival, but I didn't add that.

I left Jackson behind, politely excusing myself to follow Aiden to the kids' section. When I reached him, I pointed to the train set in the aisle. "Play with the trains for a minute. I'll be right back. I want a book. Don't make a mess," I warned.

I noticed Jackson checking on me from the end of a row, a smile on his face.

I smiled back. Never an overly boisterous person, my shyness prevented me from starting a conversation with him. Without my friends to provide moral support, I kept to myself. Back home I was never the kind of girl to start random conversations with people.

A short time later, with two books for me and one for Aiden, we waved goodbye to our new acquaintance.

"Come back anytime," Jackson said as he walked us to the door. "Welcome to town, by the way."

The hardware store was our next stop. Mom needed me to buy a hammer, nails, and cleaning supplies, and I had to ask about a new water heater. The owners, a husband and wife team, answered my questions about home repair. They ordered an appropriate water heater, and luckily it was in the closest major city so it would arrive on Monday. Until then, we'd have to boil water for warm baths.

After talking with them, I felt a small flicker of hope that Mom and I could manage a few things around the house by ourselves—and if not, their staff was skilled at home repair. "We're a one-stop-shop," the wife said as she rang me up. She chuckled. "You kind of have to be in this small of a town. If you decide that you want a hand out there, just let us know."

I agreed, and on our way out of the store, Aiden complained of hunger. A quick lunch and another stop for groceries ended our trip into town.

As I pulled onto the road back home, I thought about our house with a name and a cemetery out back. The idea of a whole summer ahead of me fixing a remote house with nothing fun to do didn't make me joyful.

***

Back at the house, movers busily unloaded the van and carried boxes inside. Mom stood issuing orders like a traffic cop. I didn't want to be in the way. The best place for my brother and I was somewhere out of reach.

"Come on, little man. Let's play."

Aiden trailed me to the spare bedroom. With the playroom as my excuse to hide away from the chaos of furniture and boxes, I unpacked a few toys and gave them to my brother. Together we set up a racetrack, and once Aiden was happily playing with cars, I figured it was a safe time to venture out and make my way downstairs.

From the looks of things, it would've been better to stay in the bedroom. Our old apartment back home was small. Once Dad left, we ended up in a two-bedroom apartment. I didn't remember so many boxes loaded into the van before we left. Where had all this stuff come from?

I felt overwhelmed with how to unpack everything and put it all away.

At least now with plenty of room for our belongings, the house was big enough so we wouldn't be living on top of each other. Aiden had room to run and play without bothering people above or below us.

I found Mom in the kitchen unpacking dishes. "Aiden's playing in his room." I unwrapped glasses from the nearest box to be helpful. "He has toys to play with. He should be fine for a little bit."

"Thanks for taking care of him. How did you like the town?" Mom stopped her chores to talk to me. "I wonder if it's changed since I was here last. I'll have to see for myself soon."

"It's small." I didn't bother adding our trip to town ended quickly because we had nothing to do.

"Give it a chance. We have few options right now," she reminded me with a slight hopeful smile. "Once we settle in, we'll be okay. This will be a good place for us."

Not ready to believe her words, I changed the topic.

"We went to the bookstore and got a couple of books. A guy named Jackson works there. He was nice. The bookstore wasn't bad."

"Good." Mom sighed at the state of the kitchen. "This does suck. I'm sorry. Things will improve. Give us a chance to settle in. You might learn to like it here."

I kept myself from disagreeing with her. *Because you say something a million times doesn't make it true. Either we win the lottery or Dad decides to work a real job and pay child support.* Neither of which I saw in the near or distant future.

Seeing her face fall when I didn't agree with her statement, I vowed to be nicer. It wasn't her fault we were in this predicament, I reminded myself. She tried hard to provide for us. "I bought fried chicken and potatoes for dinner," I said. "No need to cook tonight."

Mom laughed. I was horrible in the kitchen if food couldn't be microwaved. "I am so glad. I'm still trying to find all the pots and pans."

"We can have cereal and milk for breakfast again. Gives us one less worry."

With a sigh, Mom continued. "Between the two of us, we need to make this place livable by Sunday night. My work starts on Monday, and I don't want to be living out of boxes all week."

"I'll take Aiden's things to his room to unpack then start on my room later," I told her. "Gives us two days to finish getting the house ready. If the movers put the boxes in the right room, that would be helpful. We can get all the unpacking done. Besides, I can work on stuff this week while you're gone."

Mom started work full time and Aiden would stay home with me until school started, so I wanted the house settled too before the end of summer. Having one month before school started helped. Once junior year began at the high school, there wouldn't be time to get the house organized. I didn't want the stress of starting a strange school, making new friends, and the chaos of setting up a house at the same time.

I directed the movers to transport boxes and furniture up to the third story, trying to hurry the process up.

An hour later, with my clothes hung up in the closet and books lined up on shelves, my room seemed livable. Next, I went down to Aiden's bedroom to tackle more boxes. For a little boy, Aiden owned more items than I did. Putting them away took longer than I expected.

Later, Mom and I had our first normal conversation without anger since leaving California. With her at the kitchen table, talking and planning made me feel useful helping make decisions for our family.

"How about a bookshelf in his room? Put the old toy box in the spare. List everything we need. The hardware store will deliver for us," Mom said.

"They will?"

"Small town. People are willing to help here. The hardware store's delivered for the past fifty years, at least as far as I remember."

Her comment jogged my memory. "The lady that works there said that they help with home repairs," I blurted. "Maybe they can deliver us a handyman to help with things. There's so much to repair. Most of it I didn't know how to fix."

Mom nodded. "Make a list of everything we want and another for what needs to be fixed right away. We can figure out what's important and prioritize."

"It's only going to be finished if we either wave a magic wand or hire help." I stuck my tongue out in jest. "We can always hope."

"We'll do what we can on our own. You can learn to be a plumber." She laughed at the disgust on my face. She knew half the time I couldn't walk without tripping. Mom probably didn't want me near anything that could cause a flood in the house.

As we talked, Aiden walked in, interrupting our banter. "Mommy, can I have cups of water? Two of them?"

"Two? Why would you need two?" Mom asked. "Are you extra thirsty?"

"Nope," Aiden said. "One is for my friend. She wants one."

"A friend?" Mom looked at me quizzically, her eyes wide with surprise. "What's her name? I didn't realize anyone came for a visit."

I shrugged. There was no one but us in the house now that the movers had left.

"I forgot her name. But can I?" He walked to the cupboards and stared at us blankly. I almost laughed—of course he wouldn't know which cupboard the glasses were in.

"All right," Mom said, rising to her feet. "Hope you're thirsty." She filled two cups and handed them to him. "Don't spill. Give me a minute and I'll make a snack for you, little man."

Curious to see his playmate, I followed Aiden to the playroom. It was empty.

"Where's your friend?"

"I don't know." He picked up a car. "She left."

"What'd she look like?"

"She's got blond hair and a green dress." He set the cups on the windowsill and went back to playing with cars. "She's pretty." Distracted by his toys, he made no more mention of his friend.

To keep him company I sat on his bed and worked on the to-do list. Once finished, I searched for Mom before I found her putting the last of her personal items away in her bedroom. There was the matter of the backyard to discuss.

"Mom, can we talk for a minute?"

"Sure." She sat on the bed next to me.

"You realize graves are out back?" I sounded like a scared five-year-old. "Why didn't you mention that?"

"Sadie, I had a lot on my mind with the move." She shrugged as if cemeteries out back held no significance. "It's been decades since I've been here. I forgot about them."

"You forgot about a cemetery? *Seriously*?"

"Remember, I only came here once for a few months in the summer to stay with my aunt and uncle right after my parents died while the family decided what to do with me. They were pleasant enough. But when I went to live with Aunt Rachel and Uncle Max full time, I didn't see them again. I never had a reason to come back until now."

"Still doesn't explain how you forgot a detail like that."

Now quiet, Mom appeared thoughtful. "The cemetery was built a long time ago. We'll keep your brother out. I don't need him getting hurt by falling gravestones." She paused. "The last relative lived here four years ago with some renters. There's money in a trust, enough to keep the place running. We have a safe home now. That's what I want for us."

One hundred and seventy-two years was a lot of family history to lose. The conversation reminded me of Jackson's comments earlier at the bookstore. "Why is the place named Roselynn?"

"My aunt told me a story once how the original owner planted roses after a daughter named Lynn was born. So they combined Rose and Lynn," Mom answered. "That's all I remember. I was young and paid no attention."

"I can make a trip to the library. Since we live here, it'd be interesting to know about the house." I might as well learn about the place if I was going to be stuck here.

"You always want to learn everything."

"You never know what you'll find out." Maybe I could find ancient treasures buried here. It would make life more interesting.

"Enough sitting around here!" Mom jumped from the bed. "Go rest. We're up early tomorrow. With one day left before I start my first half-day of work, we need to finish what we can."

***

With my own things unpacked, my room started to look comfortable.

As I crawled into bed and pulled bed covers over myself, the scent of roses filled the room. I paused, wondering where it might be coming from. The smell caused me to question whether to leave the bed or not and search for the source.

No roses grew out back, I knew. I pulled the covers away and checked the front yard from my window, but unfortunately it was too dark to tell what flowers were there. I'd have to wait until morning to get a better look.

Gazing out onto the pitch-black yard from the window began to creep me out and I ran back to bed.

# Chapter 4

Sunday morning came, bringing the smell of frying bacon and Aiden's laughter into my room. Based on the noise and aromas making their way up my floor, Mom had gotten up early to fix breakfast. After eating junk food on the trip, I was glad to see Mom cooking again and hurried to join them.

In the kitchen, my stomach growled at the sight of pancakes, orange juice, bacon, and oatmeal laid out on the table. Mom and Aiden were already helping themselves to everything, so I grabbed some before the food disappeared.

"Mommy's funny. She came and sang to me last night. Then she forgot she did it," Aiden remarked around a mouthful of bacon.

I looked at Mom quizzically. "What's going on?"

She shrugged. "He says I came into his room and sang him a song. Then tucked him in. I didn't."

"She's funny." He shoved pancake pieces into his mouth, oblivious to Mom's exasperation.

I tried to be helpful. "Mom, did you sleepwalk? Or you dreamed it?" I turned to Aiden to make a joke of the situation. "She isn't old enough to be forgetful yet."

"He dreamed it. Can we eat now? There's a lot to do today." Mom stopped the discussion, irritated with the topic. "We need to eat and start work."

An hour later, chore list in hand, I left for the hardware store. In addition to picking up some things for more repairs—the toilet downstairs had started leaking—I was to make an appointment to have a handyman come out and give us a bid on the most important projects: re-grouting the bathroom tiles that were cracked and falling off, stained ceilings that indicated that the roof leaked in places, and finding a solution to drafty windows. Mom told me to come back quickly. That order wasn't difficult to follow—there wasn't much to do in town—so I returned home with everything from my list that would fit in the car. I was also told that our new hot water heater would be delivered later that day.

\*\*\*

Unpacking boxes and rearranging furniture left me grubby and not in the best condition to meet new people. If I knew a guy my age would be ringing our doorbell later with supplies, I would have changed my clothes or put on some makeup.

At the door, a teenage boy not much older than myself greeted me. With sandy-colored hair, a welcoming smile, and light blue eyes, he made me wish I didn't resemble an awful mess.

"Hi. I'm Tristan," he introduced himself with a big grin.

I stood like a silent idiot, covered in dust, too embarrassed with my appearance to respond.

"I'm here with your delivery," he went on, motioning to the water heater behind him. He waited to be invited in, a lopsided smile on his face. "I'm supposed to work on the house," he added when I didn't open the door farther.

I snapped out of my fog and stopped making a spectacle of myself. "Sorry. Come in. I'm Sadie. Let me find Mom." I left him in the entryway and hurried away to cover my embarrassment.

After introductions and a short discussion, Mom decided to put me in charge of our helper while he installed the new water heater. Afterward, I showed him around the house, pointing out the repairs that needed to be made.

"You did a quick job for only being here a couple of days." Tristan motioned to the stack of empty moving boxes piled by the front door.

"The house got pretty cleaned up before we came," I said. "Movers unloaded everything from the truck. Mom and I need to finish unpacking and put everything away."

Tristan paused at the back door. "Your backyard needs work. A Boy Scout troop could make this a community service project. The yard can be cleaned up in no time."

"I can start on it this week while Mom works. Thanks though." No way did I want him to think we needed charity. We might not have been able to afford a lot of things right then, but we didn't need a bunch of strangers doing work for free.

"It'll take more than a week to make it safe. My brother's troop wants to earn more badges," Tristan pressed, trying to convince me. "It really is no problem."

"I'll ask my mom." I ended the topic, not wanting to go into detail about why my family didn't have extra money for hiring too much extra help. School would be bad if it got around town my family was poor before people had a chance to know me.

I listened to Tristan ask questions about what we wanted to be fixed, but my mind was elsewhere. Having a friend on the first day of school would be great if Tristan stayed as nice as he seemed.

Then Tristan steered the conversation in an unexpected direction and I stopped thinking about making friends.

"You seen the ghost yet?"

*Should I be surprised?* Not knowing if he was joking, I laughed. "No."

"This place is haunted by a ghost lady in the cemetery. She's been spotted in your backyard too."

With this information I would close the blinds every night. That was all the house needed—trespassers and ghost sightings.

"Great."

Everyone knows ghosts appear in cemeteries. But I wasn't keen on one appearing in the backyard. The idea of actual ghosts this close gave me shivers.

"She's been up in the top room too," he added, with a smile on his face when we made our way upstairs. He stared at me, waiting for my reaction. "Not that I have."

I wouldn't sleep at night knowing a ghostly figure might wake me. Maybe I should ask Mom for an extra night light or a different room to sleep in.

My silence, as I contemplated my response, ended up interpreted as a sign of interest and he continued with enthusiasm. "A girl in this house killed herself after learning her boyfriend died in the Civil War. Her ghost haunts the place, waiting for him."

"That's original." I rolled my eyes. "Like that story hasn't been repeated a million times before." I didn't want to hear about ghosts anymore. "Come on, finish walking the rest of the house. You can talk to Mom about everything afterward." I pushed him out of my room.

My mind whirled with questions about my new house. But hesitant to discuss it with a stranger, I said nothing. I left him with Mom to discuss his list and went back to my room to dwell on what he told me.

***

At dinner, Mom and I went over the calendar for the week. I didn't mention Tristan's unusual conversation. There was enough for her to worry about without thinking we moved to the setting of a scary movie.

"Tristan will come back tomorrow. I called his mother about the Boy Scout troop working on the backyard. I think they can come. They need a community project and we need the help," Mom said. "The sooner we straighten the house up, the better."

"I'll do my best to help. We might run out of food if there's a lot of people," I said, worried. "Hope they like peanut butter and jelly sandwiches."

"Do what you can. Find out how many people he thinks will come when he arrives tomorrow. Call me tomorrow at work. I can always pick up some food at the store on the way home tonight."

Before Mom came to put Aiden to bed, I gently questioned him about his disappearing friend. Tristan's announcement of a resident ghost alongside Aiden's invisible friend left me unsettled.

"Do you like it here?" I asked as I helped with his pajamas.

"I can play in the backyard on the swing. Mommy told me. The nice lady came last night and tucked me in."

"What is she like?" With Aiden's imagination, I didn't know whether he was a lonely little boy who made things up, or if he actually thought he had an invisible friend.

"She wore a long dress. How come you never wear dresses, Sadie?" He innocently held a stuffed bear.

"I like jeans. Besides, I'm going to need to wear them to clean up the backyard. The yard is a mess." I picked him up and placed him on the bed so we could talk. "She came last night?"

"She's sad. She doesn't smile. Are you happy?" he asked. He acted as if strange people in bedrooms were perfectly normal.

"I am." *I do admit to getting a tad worried that you insist someone comes at night to tuck you in.*

Aiden fell asleep cuddled up with his favorite stuffed animal. Kissing the top of his head, I whispered good night to him. One last glance around the darkened room didn't reveal anything out of the ordinary.

That night, my first dream about the house and former occupants came.

I didn't know it, but it signaled the first of many dreams, the start of everything.

# Chapter 5

I found myself surrounded by injured, dying men all who wore torn blue uniforms. These men were Yankees—they were from the north. They didn't belong here. They would die in the South.

At least fifty men lay scattered around the front yard and porch. Body parts missing on some, all hurt. Everyone smeared with blood from wounds and injuries. Men begged for help. A few tried to sit up, reaching weakly for me. Others too wounded to do anything lifted a hand or turned their head in my direction.

Some appeared dead, their bodies still, no movement visible to give any indication of life left in them.

Outfitted in a long green dress, with tall black lace-up shoes, I wore the kind of clothing only seen in time period movies. In the chaos, finding myself wearing a dress splattered with blood on the bodice and hem caused a surreal sensation within me.

I walked down the nearest row of men, unsure what to do. With no one else around to offer help or direct me in this nightmare of death, I was paralyzed. Who should I assist first? I fought the urge to cry from helplessness. They all looked to need immediate attention.

One little boy, no more than ten years old, called for his mother. I reassured him he would be all right.

"Momma," he mumbled softly. Seconds ticked by until his breathing quieted.

I cried.

At each man, I promised to find help; they only needed to hang on a little bit longer until I brought someone. The final man, propped up against a tree, suffered a gash in his left leg. His blanched face conveyed hopelessness. I feared him dead. As I got closer, the palest blue eyes slowly opened, staring back at me.

I didn't know it then that this soldier, although 153 years dead, would become an important part of my life.

I immediately woke, finding myself back in bed. The room appeared the same as when I fell asleep, but I didn't feel normal. Disoriented and confused with a rapidly beating heart, I expected men and chaos to surround me, not the quiet darkness.

I fought the urge to flee my room and throw myself into Mom's bed, begging to spend the rest of the night with her.

*** 

In the morning, I found Mom ready to leave for work. After I ate and got dressed, the dream had lost its terrible hold over me.

A knock on the front door brought ten little Boy Scouts and four moms to help for the day. The boys, a lively bunch, followed directions given by their supervisors. A nonstop busy morning of gardening made the time pass while Aiden and I helped clean up the yard with them.

Four hours into the day, ten garbage bags full of weeds and dead branches revealed long-forgotten flower beds and walkways.

When the group took a break for lunch, I was faced with the possibility that someone had information about my new surroundings. I asked the small group of women about the house and town.

Turns out the town was not as boring as I originally believed.

"This place used to be a rest stop for traders on the James River. Boats traveled between Charleston and New Orleans carrying cotton, food, and slaves," one parent informed me.

"Your house used to grow cotton, like most of the other plantations around here. Until the war," someone interjected.

"When the battle happened, wounded soldiers were dumped at the different houses and the town. Your house was one of them," another voice spoke. "Roselynn was commandeered by Union troops and turned into a hospital."

What I saw in my dream matched this new information, but it didn't explain what I experienced with the strangers. I was speechless, stunned by a dream that turned out to mirror reality. *I can't believe the house we're living in played an important part in the Civil War.* It was bizarre to have learned about the Civil War a few years earlier in elementary and middle school, and see the places firsthand now—not to mention *live in* one of these history-rich places.

"What happened afterward?" I asked.

"The town and most of the houses fell into disrepair. The land got sold off piece by piece."

With the afternoon drawing to a close, the volunteers informed me they would be back to plant flowers. I tried to talk them out of coming back, but they reassured me everything was already taken care of. Since there was no point in arguing with them, I thanked them as each mother gave me a hug.

Tristan, finished with work for the day, left soon after Aiden and I had the house to ourselves.

One phone call to Mom to tell her about the progress and then Aiden and I went off for a walk.

The woods behind the house were not terribly thick. The trees spread out enough to let sunlight through patches. Along an old dirt footpath, I reminded Aiden to stay close and not get lost. With his imagination running wild, he soon let go of my hand and set about exploring.

While he poked around the dirt making a racetrack for his cars, I pictured men fighting in the woods as war raged around them. In the quiet, I found it hard to imagine the chaos that once took place here.

I spied a rose bush at the base of one tree, and a riot of pink color in full bloom contrasted the rest of the forest. As I got closer, its smell reminded me of the one in my room.

We walked home, and I was deep in thought the entire way.

***

The next morning, I tackled my chore list for cleaning the house. Dusting was the easy part since we didn't own a whole lot of furniture to dust. Vacuuming the wooden floor proved harder—the ancient vacuum cleaner barely worked. In my room, the wood floor didn't want to be cleaned easily. I wiped the floor with a mop I found in the downstairs closet.

One small piece of flooring in the closet felt higher than the rest. I tried to squish the wood down, but the piece refused to fit back into place.

I knelt down and used my fingernails to lift it up, but they weren't long enough. With a knife from downstairs slipped into the crevice, I popped the piece out of place and found a small dark hole large enough to slip my hand through. With a silent prayer of not touching bugs or anything with fur, I reached in…and pulled out a small wooden box.

Six inches long, the rectangular object was stained a muddy brown. Someone had fashioned a delicate wooden rose to the top of the box. Two tiny hinges on the back of the lid and a small latch on the front allowed the lid to open easily.

Inside was a silver oval locket on a delicate chain. On the front a floral pattern; on the back the initials *L.H.*; an empty space designed to fit two small pictures inside.

One last check in the cavity turned up nothing. After setting the flooring back in place, I set the newly discovered items on my bookshelf.

Later I showed Mom when she returned from work. "Look what I found." I held out the locket and box.

"Where'd you find them?" She took off her glasses to give both a closer look.

"Hidden under the floor by the closet. One of the floorboards was a little out of place." I sheepishly left out the part of using a knife to pry the wood up. "This came out."

"I've never seen this necklace." Ever the responsible person, Mom worried about the damage I might have inflicted on the house. "Did you ruin the floor?"

"Nope. I put the piece back. You can't tell the difference."

Mom returned her attention to the necklace. "I guess you can keep it. I would be interested to know who it belonged to." Mom returned the box and locket to me.

"I wouldn't know how to find out." I was glad to keep the jewelry and not be in trouble for pulling up the flooring.

"Well, it's probably pretty old, not something to wear every day. It would be a shame to break it."

"I'll keep it in the box for now. Maybe someone can appraise or clean it?" While the necklace was not worth a million dollars, I wanted to take care of it.

"When I'm in town tomorrow, I'll ask if anyone can look it over. Be careful." With one last hug goodnight, Mom sent me away so she could sleep.

I set the box on my dresser. What other discoveries were hidden in this house? All I learned about Roselynn's history made me curious to find out more.

# Chapter 6

Dreams returned that night, but not soldiers left for dead on the front lawn this time. Instead, a young lady invaded my sleep.

In my room, I gazed out the window with its view of the backyard and a fountain. The yard burst with flowers, full of blooming color sprays everywhere. Beyond the wall, a few graves stood at attention in the cemetery. They didn't look forlorn or forgotten, no longer chipped or cracked. The surrounding trees, much smaller in stature and clearly less mature, left gravestones unharmed. Beyond the cemetery stood a cluster of small cabins, hidden in the trees.

Off in the distance, a small group of black men and women walked rows of plants. Bent over picking cotton, women wore large-brimmed straw hats that did little to keep the burning midday sun off their tired faces. Enormous baskets with white fluffs appeared too heavy to be carried for long. The women's dresses seemed bulky and uncomfortable for farming.

*Slaves*, I realized.

Their movements held my attention until the bedroom door flew open behind me. I glanced over my shoulder to see a blonde girl run by in a green blur and throw herself on the bed. She sobbed loudly and acted like I was invisible. In the shock of her unexpected appearance, I reached out to comfort her.

I woke up to my bedroom in pitch-black darkness and the smell of roses.

*A blond-haired girl in a green dress*, I thought. *Aiden's playmate?*

Sighing, I pulled the quilt over my shoulders and rolled over. The girl in distress was better than dying soldiers.

\*\*\*

In the morning, I pinpointed the location of the cabins I had seen in my dream. I wanted to make sure to get to the right spot since I planned to take Aiden on another walk.

More surprises greeted me when the knock came for our morning yard helpers. Teenagers stood on the porch to join the workgroup. Big brothers came to help out the little brothers as Tristan brought his friends. A short conversation explained that his friends felt bad their moms and little brothers worked hard and they were not.

I wasn't one to complain about extra help after the progress from yesterday. I happily directed everyone out back. Aiden and I worked on the front porch cleaning the first-floor windows.

The number of people willing to help complete strangers surprised me. Hearing all the noise and laughter of the helpers pushed unhappy thoughts away and got me out of my post-move funk. Maybe it wouldn't be so bad here, after all. People were much more friendly here than where we lived in California.

Lunch once again provided enough food for an army. This time Aiden ate with the Boy Scouts, giving Tristan a chance to introduce me to his group of high school friends.

It was fun to be with others my own age. His three friends spent part of the time discussing plans to make their senior year unforgettable. Somehow, the conversation turned to my resident ghost, how I liked living with her. Since Aiden wasn't close by, I answered what I could.

"Tristan said something about a ghost. But I haven't seen one," I admitted. "Have any of you?"

"Heck no. But everyone knows about her," a boy named Charles said.

"Who's the ghost?" I asked.

"The girl who used to live here. She killed herself, upset her boyfriend died in the Civil War."

I swallowed. "How did she kill herself?"

"Some people say she did the deed with poison. Some say she hung herself from a tree," someone else in the group offered.

Another boy added, "No, she was murdered."

I couldn't ask anything further when Aiden walked by needing to use the bathroom.

***

The afternoon passed in a blur as our maintenance crew of helpers finished their jobs in the backyard, leaving no time for more questions. The brick wall, once a broken mess but now patched and repaired, enhanced the beauty of our new backyard. Green plants and blossoming flowers completed the sanctuary for my family.

I didn't get any more chances to ask Tristan's friends about the girl who once lived in my house. The visitors had piqued my interest in the tales of a girl that no one confirmed how she died, yet all the contradicting versions made little sense.

With everyone gone and the house quiet, I had nothing to distract me from our resident ghost. Watching cartoons with Aiden wasn't stimulating enough.

I took the two of us for a walk out to the trees behind the house, where I looked for evidence of the slave cabins. A five-minute stroll and we arrived at the general location of the cabins. Not much remained of either building. A few rotten wooden boards piled on the ground may have been from anything.

A pathway formed from two rows of rocks might once have been the front entrance of a dwelling. Another area reminded me of a vegetable garden, though nothing grew now. Between dismantled buildings and the amount of time that had passed, nothing remained for me now to discover. Whether they were slave cabins like my dream suggested, or just my overactive imagination playing tricks, I didn't know.

As Aiden and I walked away, I wondered how my dreams knew buildings stood in the spot. How could I know to walk here, specifically here, if my dreams were not accurate?

Such thoughts kept me silent as I walked Aiden back to the house.

# Chapter 7

I spent the week taking care of Aiden and organizing the house. Mom let me take the car into town for a few hours Saturday, saying I deserved a break and time to myself.

My first stop was the library to research the house and its history.

The inside looked like any other library I visited, except for the many photographs the library framed and displayed for visitors. Along with numerous shelves of books, the walls were decorated with pictures of the town. A visual parade of former residents and celebrations documented the long history of Falls Creek. The earliest ones, dated 1849, depicted the town's founding fathers. Most showed stuffy old men looking solemn at the front of the courthouse. The celebrations of new buildings, swearings-in of elected officials, and store openings were all commemorated and framed to fill the wall space.

It wasn't long before I came across a picture of Roselynn.

Seeing the house in good condition with no peeling paint or scraggly trees shocked me. At one point, the house resembled a showpiece. Too bad the picture couldn't be done in color. A metal plaque read: *General Hamilton and household. Falls Creek, North Carolina, May 1862.*

On the steps leading up to the front door sat a small group of individuals. The enlarged photograph in shades of black, white, and gray made the image blurry. Based on the clothing style, the family didn't appear raggedy or poor. In the center of the picture, a bearded man wore a gray military uniform and hat. Confederate. He appeared serious, and was the most formally dressed of the group. He gave no hint of a smile. I guessed he was General Hamilton since he appeared the oldest in the group.

Two younger men sat on each side of him. One of them wore a military style similar to General Hamilton; the other man wore a long jacket and pants. This one appeared more relaxed and less stern. Two middle-aged women in long-sleeved dresses sat on the steps below the men. Wide-brimmed hats partially blocked their faces, making their expressions impossible to figure out.

A young boy and a teenage girl on the lowest row stared directly at the camera. The boy's face reminded me of Aiden when he tried hard to be quiet but couldn't quite succeed. The girl, her hair parted in the middle and pulled back in a bun, smiled. The style of the dress was reminiscent of the sobbing girl who ran into my room, although I didn't get enough of a look in my dream to distinguish between the two, and I couldn't see if her dress was green as it had been in my dream. A shaggy little dog completed the family scene.

With only General Hamilton named, I had little clue of the residents who once lived in the house.

The progression of photos continued parading the citizens of the town, but none showed the house or its occupants again.

With nothing else useful found hanging on the wall, I went to the librarian's desk to ask about the local history. Actual books might give more accurate information than hand-me-down stories contradicting each other.

The librarian, whose name was Evelyn, was a stereotypical little old lady with gray hair and glasses, and wore a long dress. What wasn't stereotypical was her loud, boisterous personality that didn't fit her shrunken body. After explaining how I wanted to research my family, she got right to work tracking down information.

At the section devoted to North Carolina and Falls Creek history, Evelyn gave a quick rundown on each of the books she deemed important for my search. Soon enough I learned which author wrote what, why the book was published, and which ones were written "so full of lies" that she forbade me to check them out and waste my time. Based on this, I walked away with three of her favorites, excited to see what I could find out.

I stopped at the hardware store next to talk to Tristan about when to schedule the remaining repairs. Now that Mom and I had been in the house a short time, we had a better idea of what we wanted fixed first. Since Mom was working, we could be a little more liberal with our money for repairs, but honestly, the home repairs were taking more time and money than we anticipated.

With the supply list taken care of for Mom, and arrangements made for the rest of the work, I headed to the diner for a quiet lunch by myself. Inside, Jackson sat at a booth, book in hand. It took me a moment to place him as one of the first people I met, the teenager who worked at the bookstore. I waved but requested the waitress sit me farther away. I had no reason to appear pushy and make a bad impression.

As I flipped through the library books, I noticed him standing at the side of my table. "Mind if I join you for a minute?" He brushed his brown hair out of his eyes. One glance at the book in my hand and he said, "I don't want to disturb you."

Always shy with strangers, especially cute ones, I closed the book and gave him a slight smile. "Sure, have a seat and join me."

"How do you like your new place so far?" Jackson slid into the booth across from me.

"I keep busy. Everything is almost unpacked. People came out and fixed the backyard. Aiden has a place to play now. He's happy."

"I heard. Nothing like a football team doing community service." His tone was unfriendly.

"We need all the help we can get," I said, taken aback by his attitude. *What?*

"Sorry. I'm sure you can use the help," he said, backpedaling. "Nice of them to volunteer."

I stared at him. "Why do you hate them so much? Have you seen our house? You must know it needs work."

"I work in a bookstore. They don't read much." He gave no further explanation.

Not wanting to cause hurt feelings with kind people who had gone out of their way to be helpful, I changed the direction of the conversation. "You worked there long?"

"My parents own the store, so I always work there."

"Must be nice to have a job." I thought of my own rapidly depleting funds and wondered how much longer the money would last. Since the move, I had done no babysitting jobs to earn extra money.

"Pays for college."

"You're in college?" I said. Jackson looked as young as I did.

"Summer break. I help out to give my parents time off from running the store. You should stop by again. We got new stuff in you might be interested in."

"I don't save enough money to buy all the books I want." If I had my way, my bedroom walls would be lined with books waiting to be read.

"Come work at the bookstore," he offered. "Part-time anyway. There's an employee discount, if that helps with your decision."

"I'm watching Aiden while Mom works during the day. Between babysitting him and not having a car, it's hard to find a job." Images of biking to work filled my head, replaced with me on the side of the road injured with no one to help. *No thank you.*

"My parents want to slow down and take some time off. I'm taking a couple of online classes in a few weeks to get an early start on the semester. Come on weekends. It would help everyone out. Mom and Pop talk all the time about having some more help. I'll need some time to study."

"Don't they have to interview me or something? I need to run things by Mom first anyway." It would be embarrassing to show up one day and they had no idea who I was.

"You like books. If you're good with a computer and can punch numbers on a keyboard to ring up sales, you'll be fine."

"If you trained me, I probably could," I admitted.

Still not sure, but liking the idea of a paying job and money, I agreed to talk with Mom about working part-time in his shop. If she agreed, I would talk to his parents.

***

After a short discussion later that night, Mom agreed to me working weekends if the owners approved. She would drop me off and pick me up, which would leave her to use the car to run her own errands.

Bedtime became eerily quiet as Aiden and Mom slept in their own rooms. With no neighbors next door, the usual sounds of traffic, TVs, and conversations were missing. I thought about calling a couple of friends back home, but hearing about all the fun they were having this summer wouldn't make me feel any better, or less lonely.

With Aiden seeing someone in the house and townspeople insisting the place was haunted, I figured I was due to observe this mysterious ghost. She added excitement to my life, I had to admit. Maybe it would also add excitement to my evening.

In bed, I waited in the dark for something to fill the silence. I wanted voices of people walking their dogs, cars driving by, or kids playing basketball in the street. But nothing made me feel like a part of the world, to chase the loneliness away.

# Chapter 8

The next few weeks filled themselves with the routine of babysitting Aiden, chores around the house, and helping Tristan with repairs. Weekends working at the bookstore gave me a little extra spending money, and for the first time since moving here, Mom and I felt as if we could finally breathe.

And above all...my sleep brought soldiers again.

The blue-eyed soldier from the front yard lay on a pallet in the downstairs living room, which had been emptied of furniture to give space to the recovering men. A bowl of food was in his hands, and he ate hungrily. The girl was busy, bustling between the injured soldiers, caring for them, but she stopped in front of the blue-eyed soldier. She seemed to be the only one in charge at the house. She walked around with an air of nervous authority, as if she lived here but was doing something wrong.

*Well, if she did live here, her loyalties should have been with the Confederates, not the Union soldiers.* Yet here she was, caring for the injured and dying men regardless of the uniforms they wore. Who was she?

Once the bowl was emptied, the Union soldier whispered to the girl, "Thank you, Lynn."

One piece of the puzzle dropped into place. If everything I knew was right, and the girl who lived here was the daughter of General Hamilton, then her name was Lynn Hamilton.

*L.H.*, I remembered. *The initials on the locket.*

As the weeks passed, sleep became an endless movie screen of the blue-eyed solider and the girl called Lynn. I started keeping a notebook by my bed so I could write down the scenes from my dreams to remember them better.

*Lynn by herself filling a basket of flowers picked from the backyard.*
*Lynn helping in the kitchen.*
*Lynn playing with her brother — the same brother I saw in the photograph at the library!*

These were the dreams that filled my nights, and that filled my notebook.

Time passed. The soldier's injuries healed.

*The blue-eyed man used a crutch to check on those still injured.*

Daily life in 1865 played out before me, with the wounded soldiers the only oddity in an otherwise normal house. The soldier healed and began helping Lynn more and more. Over time, I watched as the relationship between

Lynn and her soldier changed. They spoke more words to each other, and their formality gave way to togetherness. I watched from afar as the girl fell in love with the soldier boy.

*But who are they? And why are they in my dreams?* These questions filled the pages of my notebook.

The next dream started ordinarily enough. Lynn and the soldier sat under the shade of a tree in the backyard. Lynn sewed a piece of fabric, a soft smile on her face. The soldier, his leg still bandaged, read out loud from a book as she listened. He paused, gazing at her.

"Keep reading Daniel, please."

His name was Daniel.

Another piece of the puzzle in place. Lynn Hamilton and Daniel, a Yankee soldier. A forbidden love between a girl of the South and a boy from the North. I sighed in relief, knowing that this was the first bit of information I could leverage to find out who these lovers were—and why they haunted my dreams.

\*\*\*

With my regular group of friends on the other side of the country, my summer was wide open. No plans. Nothing to do. Perhaps that's why I was so adamant about wanting to solve this mystery.

Well, and the fact that I didn't particularly enjoy ghosts haunting my dreams. Or tucking Aiden in at night.

Secrets didn't pop out in plain sight as I searched for evidence of the girl named Lynn Hamilton. I looked for cracks in the wood floors, for hidden compartments like the jewelry box and necklace. I checked every enclosed space in the house. Hours of searching yielded not a single scrap of anything. In fact, nothing was accomplished except a clean house. My work made Mom happy, me not so much. I was no closer to finding anything. Just sick of cleaning as my excuse to snoop.

One of the few things I had to go on was the smell of roses. That and Lynn had to be connected, somehow. Why else would the smell of roses appear after my ghostly dreams?

With everyone telling me the ghost appeared in my room, I decided to appeal to her directly from there. "What do you want? Point me in the right direction. What do you need me to do?" I said from the doorway.

I expected no answer to come out of thin air. Ghosts can't talk back.

\*\*\*

That night, she responded. My dream started with me standing in the dining room looking out the window, the sky outside glowing pink with the setting sun. The aroma of dinner cooking was strong enough to make my stomach growl.

Soldiers gathered around a table in the dining room. Poring over a map, they discussed military strategies on which direction their troops should move. Other men stood guard at the front door of the house. Others calmly went about their various tasks. And this was it—a snapshot of 1865, of the soldiers preparing to defend what their half of the country believed in.

When I woke up, early morning sunrise peeked through the window, filling the bedroom with light. On my dresser, I spied the jewelry box. I had put it on my bookshelf days ago.

*Who moved the jewelry box?*

It was too high for Aiden to reach. Mom, rarely home with her busy work schedule, would have woken me up if she came in my room at night. Nobody could have moved the jewelry box. *Nobody could have moved it.*

But deep in my heart I knew. It was a sign from Lynn.

That afternoon I made a list of questions. Why was Lynn here? Why did I have nightly dreams? Why did she move the jewelry box and the locket that once belonged to her? And above all: How was I supposed to help Lynn? Too many unanswered questions made me more determined to find answers.

A ghost existed in the house. With the strange things happening, I could not deny her existence.

\*\*\*

Life continued on. Tristan helped with minor repairs in the kitchen, saving me a ton of work I couldn't do on my own. Aiden liked to stick around and watch his new friend so he could pretend to be fixing the house too. But today I sent him off.

"Remember when you told me about the ghost in my room, Tristan? What do you know?" I pressed. "For real. Not what others say."

"You've seen her? About time." Tristan put his hammer down to face me.

"Maybe."

"You got all mad when I mentioned her the first time."

"Yeah, okay, shut up. I didn't know you. I'd barely been in the house when you first brought it up."

"Her Confederate boyfriend found out she was dating a Yankee," Tristan said. "The Confederate snuck back and killed the Yank."

A new twist to the story. When would someone tell me the accurate version of events?

He frowned. "She was so upset that she killed herself."

"If he's the one who died, why is her ghost here? Besides, how do you know?"

"Stories have been passed down for years."

It still made no sense. If Daniel did get murdered, why did no one see his ghost here? Until now, no one mentioned a male being killed. The only reason I knew Daniel existed was through my dreams.

"Where'd you see her?" Tristan asked.

"I haven't. Aiden talks to a female playmate only he can see." I didn't go into detail about dreams or a hidden necklace, not ready to share them yet. If the dreams were just my overactive imagination, I didn't want Tristan to think I had problems. "I made copies of the pictures at the library. I want to see if Aiden recognizes one of the girls who lived in the house."

"What are you going to do about her?" he asked.

With everything I dreamed about and all the questions left unanswered, I didn't have an answer for him.

***

Days later I cornered Aiden about his unseen lady friend.

"Aiden, can I show you a couple of things?"

I held copies of pictures made from the library. To make sure I didn't lead him on, I included some of the Hamilton family as well as other town members.

"That's my friend." He pointed to the teenage girl in the Hamilton family picture. "She's pretty. Just like I told you."

My breath caught. Lynn was the girl in the picture and the girl in my dreams, and she was also Aiden's imaginary friend. "What's her name?"

"I forgot." Aiden went back to battling his toy cars with his dinosaurs. "Here Sadie, let's play car crash." He grabbed a car and dinosaur and ran off, oblivious to my excitement. At least Aiden's imaginary friend and the girl from my dreams were the same.

# Chapter 9

Saturday during my lunch break, I headed back to the library. I wanted to search old newspaper articles for any mention of Lynn's suicide, in the hopes they provided answers to all the unanswered questions surrounding her.

I asked Evelyn for all the newspapers the library had available related to Lynn Hamilton's death. More than happy to oblige, she tracked down all the information she could locate.

With the copies tucked into my purse for safekeeping, I didn't want to rush reading through them. I had only a few minutes of lunch remaining, and as much as it killed me to wait, I did.

At work, it took getting used to people coming to meet the new girl. Tristan's friends stopped by the store more than Jackson originally let on. People didn't stop to buy books; they chatted and passed the time. It felt good to make new friends I could joke around with. Jackson's parents lived above the shop, which allowed them to visit and keep an eye on their business. Their son didn't stop by often. College classes kept him busy.

Tristan occasionally came when in town picking up supplies for the repairs he planned to do at the house. If the store happened to be quiet, we passed the time. After my trip to the library, I was happy to see Tristan when he stopped by to check in with me. The bookstore was empty of customers and I had a quiet moment to myself.

"I made some copies from newspapers today about Lynn," I said to him.

"Does it creep you out being in the house with a ghost?" Tristan asked.

"No." I still didn't tell him about the dreams. "How come you never saw her?"

"I think people scare themselves stupid. In the dark, they hear a sound. Shadows move. Next thing you know, people freak out. I don't frighten easily." He shrugged.

"You notice anything in the house?" I prodded.

"Like what? Dead bodies?"

"Sometimes at night, I smell roses. Aiden's played in his room when things happened too." I didn't want him to believe me crazy.

"Nope. At first, I thought it would be freaky working in a haunted house. The house is normal." He laughed. "Maybe she doesn't like me."

"People talk about a ghost in my house. I haven't seen her. I find it strange."

"You're complaining about *not* seeing a ghost?"

"I want to know who and why people see strange things in my house. That can't be weird," I said.

"Guess not. Never met anybody looking for a ghost on purpose."

"You never went into the house before this?"

He shook his head for emphasis. "If any of us trespassed, all of our parents would've killed us."

"They're okay with you all hanging out in a cemetery, but you can't go into the house next to it? That doesn't make sense to me."

"After the last of the family died, the house still belonged to somebody. The sheriff gave us a talking to. He instructed us not to set foot on the property. We damaged anything, we would be responsible. He was pretty serious. We don't break the law."

I didn't bother pointing out that the cemetery and the house sat on private property. Either one would be considered trespassing. "Nice to know I'm not friends with a future jailbird," I said.

"We friends, Sadie?"

My heart beat quickly, hearing his question. "Sure we are."

"Go out with some of us Friday, then."

Surprise. I'd never had a conversation with a boy about ghosts, breaking the law, and going out all at the same time. After having worked with Tristan around the house for the past few weeks, there was no reason to be shy or nervous around him. We were friends, that's all. He saw me wearing grubby clothes often enough. I didn't worry about impressing him.

"Let me make sure Mom agrees. I can't go until she gets back from work or I'm off from the bookstore. What did you have in mind? No hanging out in the graveyard."

"Deal. I can do better than a cemetery," he promised.

The bell above the door chimed, and with a smile on my face, I let Tristan go on his way. But it made me feel good to have a friend.

When Mom and Aiden came to pick me up later that afternoon, I relayed my conversation.

"It would be nice for you to get out some. I know how hard you've been working," Mom said, sympathizing with me.

"It would be fun to be out with a friend or two," I admitted. "I haven't had a chance to hang around people my own age, unless it's at work or they come to fix the house. I want to go."

"Remember your curfew though. And I expect you to be responsible. You don't know this area," she cautioned.

I rolled my eyes. "As if I would do anything crazy."

Mom stopped at the diner, a packed and noisy affair, so different from our meals a home. It was nice to be around others who were friendly. I focused on having a fun time, without worrying about dead people.

\*\*\*

At home, I turned my attention to the articles from the library. The first turned out to be an obituary, the small and blurry letters making the information hard to read.

*Lynn Hamilton, 16, of Falls Creek, died May 10, 1865. Daughter of General George Hamilton and Emily Williams Hamilton. She was a member of the Falls Creek Baptist Church. Services to be held at Falls Creek Baptist Church on Sunday. Survivors include her mother Emily Williams Hamilton, her father George Hamilton, and brother Lowell Hamilton.*

No cause of death was listed—not murder, suicide, or illness. At least the paper verified the small boy in the picture as her sibling.

The second article, with the same print, proved as difficult to read. It's a wonder people didn't lose their eyesight reading the paper every day. This one was dated May 12, 1865.

*On Wednesday afternoon, the body of Lynn Hamilton was found in the woods behind her house. Matthew W. Sullivan was arrested here this evening upon a warrant signed by Sheriff Brown and taken to military headquarters in a closed carriage to await a hearing.*

Her death, definitely not a suicide, proved everyone's theories wrong. Nothing stated why or how her body ended up where it did. A new name was thrown into the mix, that of *a murderer*. But I never knew Matthew in my dreams.

The last article proved useless with a copy so fuzzy that only a word or two was decipherable. Not even a magnifying glass helped give any information. All I learned was it was published three days after her death.

I didn't understand why people thought Lynn killed herself. Someone was officially charged with her murder. I wondered what happened to this murderer named Matthew W. Sullivan.

With the new information, my mind was a whirl of thoughts, making sleep hard to come by. I waited in silence for something to happen, hoping for anything to take place.

Nothing.

I ended up by my window and watched the graveyard. All was quiet and uneventful. The moon gave off enough light to make gravestones visible. When I squinted into the darkness, I pictured the slave cabins in the distance. After moments of only coldness, I crawled back into bed waiting for the dreams to come.

I didn't wait long before sleep overtook me.

***

Daniel and Lynn spent time together in the forest behind the house. A blanket was spread on the ground as the two of them sat peacefully. A few feet away, the little boy from the photograph—Lowell—played with a small wooden horse. Lynn obviously loved him, as she ruffled his hair and kissed his cheek, making him giggle.

As the three interacted playfully with each other, they gave off the impression of being happy, carefree almost, as if a war wasn't being fought in their backyard. The three of them acted so casually, I fought the urge to walk over to them and shout, "What do you want from me? Why do you keep appearing in my dreams?"

A slight breeze made Lynn's hair blow into her face. Daniel reached over and brushed the long tangles off her cheeks.

The scene was interrupted when a voice called for Lynn and Lowell through the trees.

Standing as carefully as he could with an injured leg, Daniel helped Lynn to her feet. His strength unbalanced her and she stumbled slightly into him. For a moment, as she rested her head on his shoulder, I thought they would meet with a kiss, but she too hurried off, leaving Daniel alone.

He turned to me, uttering one word in the silence of the forest, easy for me to understand. "Help."

My eyes opened and I sat in bed. Again.

Great, now a female *and* a male ghost invaded my dreams. How would I help them? I lay awake in the darkness, longing to talk to my dream couple. Nothing made sense.

Eventually, the sunrise peeked through the curtains and I had a reason to get out of bed and start my day.

# Chapter 10

The next morning I didn't waste a minute lying in bed before getting dressed and heading downstairs. Before work, I walked to the graveyard to look for clues to Lynn. The house offered little in the way of answers, yet the cemetery remained uncharted territory. It made sense to come here and have a closer look…and besides, Daniel's pleading for help last night created a sense of urgency in me. His direct appeal caused feelings that I spent most of the night trying to understand.

The cemetery was surrounded by red brick walls three feet high, and one metal gate served as both entrance and exit for anyone wishing to mourn the dead. It was more decorative than functional, as most anyone would be able to climb over the short walls without difficulty. The latch itself was cracked and, unable to lock, proved useless for its designed purpose. No wonder local teenagers encountered little trouble getting in.

It wasn't a meticulously manicured final resting place like cemeteries back home. The ground, bumpy and full of weeds, made wandering around difficult. Between broken headstones and large tree roots, walking without tripping proved impossible.

The few trees within the cemetery's walls, now grown and filled out, had caused gravestones to shift positions. Green velvety moss covered the shaded tree trunks, adding to the surreal quality of the place.

Broken stones littered the ground. A few memorials tilted so far sideways that I didn't understand how they hadn't toppled over. A few headstones were damaged beyond repair, nothing more than square blocks raised above the ground. Others were so darkened with age they appeared black.

So different from my dreams when the place was cared for and maintained.

A shiver crept down my spine. All the place needed to make things perfect was a fog bank to roll in.

A small stone angel, hands clasped under her chest, gazed skyward, praying over a plot in the left corner of the land. She and her slim pedestal were shaded by tree branches near the wall—she could disappear in the shadows of nighttime. One broken wing lay on the ground in front of her.

Even despite the destruction of time, the place radiated beauty and peacefulness.

It was impossible to read any inscriptions carved into the stones—I could only decipher a letter or number by rubbing my hand over the top of headstones. Over 170 years of family history decayed and forgotten. The state of the cemetery made me sad. If I could persuade Mom to fix the place up like we had the backyard, maybe it could be presentable again.

With a sigh, I closed the gate quietly behind me.

***

At work, Jackson helped me stock a new shipment of books, but my mind was focused on the dead. Discouraged and tired, I turned to the only person available for advice. "Everyone talks about the ghost at my house."

"Yeah, what about it?" He stopped shelving books to look at me.

"How come people say she committed suicide? Information I found at the library, in old newspapers, said she was murdered."

"You went to the library?"

"Someone told me to find information on Lynn Hamilton's death. Why do people confuse the truth about what happened to her?"

"Everyone thinks they know the story growing up. It's an old tale told in school to scare people." He went back to stocking the shelves. "I tend not to listen to peoples' stories about it."

I was surprised by his unfriendly tone but continued. "Did you witness the ghost at the house?" I gave him a tense smile. "Apparently when the house was empty, it was the popular thing to do to go hang out in Roselynn's cemetery."

"I had no reason to go to high school parties in the cemetery. So I never saw anything." He shrugged. "I had no reason to go to your house." After a moment, with a smile on his face he continued, "Still no reason since I'm not invited." The teasing quality of his voice took the sting from his previous words. "Ghosts don't exist."

I grinned. "You can come anytime when I'm not working."

Since working at the store, Jackson and I had spent little time together. I ran the store while he attended summer college classes. This was the first non-hurried conversation we'd had since he'd asked me to work there. I didn't want to alienate the person who got me a job.

"Why are you asking me all of this? All the tales bothering you?" His tone switched to mild curiosity. "You should ignore the people trying to scare you."

"Would you freak out if I think my brother plays with her?" I anticipated ridicule.

"He saw her?" His eyes widened with surprise.

I explained Aiden's nighttime experiences, adding how Aiden picked her picture out of a pile of photographs.

"You shouldn't be messing with that stuff, Sadie. Who knows what you're going to uncover," he said, concerned. "Leave it alone." His eyebrows drew together in a look of anger and something else I couldn't identify.

"What do you mean?" I stepped back, stung by his comment.

"Don't you watch TV? You make ghosts angry by poking around. Any horror movie will warn you. What are you going to do? Make a ghost mad, and then what? You should leave it alone."

Mister college man worried about making a ghost mad? Not wanting to admit he made me nervous with his warnings, I convinced myself nothing would happen.

"Aiden isn't afraid of her. Who was she and what happened to her? I'm only trying to find out. That shouldn't cause problems," I said, looking away and hoping to end the conversation.

"Sadie, you aren't supposed to be digging up the past. It's too late to change things. If there's something there, you might make it mad. Think of your brother. Something might happen to him."

"I wouldn't hurt my brother for anything in the world," I said. "I only want to know what happened to her. Sorry I asked." I picked up a box of books and moved to the next aisle over to put them away.

I kept my anger to myself. Once my shift ended, I said a quick goodbye to Jackson before hurrying out the door.

\*\*\*

Later I offered to put Aiden to bed, to settle my own unease.

"Does the nice lady come to you still?"

He nodded. "She makes sure I don't get cold."

"Does she say anything to you when she comes?" If poking around for answers might stir up trouble for my brother, I would stop.

"Nope. She smiles sometimes. Then I go to sleep."

Mom came in, her hair disheveled. "Okay, Aiden, it's time for bed." She picked up his favorite stuffed animal.

An hour later, when Aiden was asleep, I asked, "Mom, when you lived here, did you ever hear about ghosts being around the house?"

"What?" She stopped folding laundry. "Where did this come from?"

I finally found the courage to talk to her about the subject, and I wasn't going to back down now. "Do you remember hearing anything about a ghost? People say one is here. Did you know?" I moved closer to her when she sat on the bed.

"The house is old with a cemetery next to it, Sadie. People talk about a ghost." She frowned. "I never gave it a thought. And nobody brought up ghosts around me. Not with my parents dead."

That made sense. No one discusses ghost hauntings with a little girl who lost her parents in a car crash and became an orphan.

She was an adult now, though, and it was a topic I wanted to discuss.

"Do you think there could be one here?" A small part of me anticipated she experienced something. "You noticed anything strange around here?"

"What are you talking about?" she said, shaking her head with surprised annoyance. "Don't tell me you listen to people gossip. They're only repeating an old tale."

"People talk about a female ghost here. I only wanted to know if they joked or not."

"Well, stop! People are trying to scare you. I don't want Aiden hearing about such stories. He'll suffer nightmares for weeks. Have the kids around here mentioned something?"

I didn't mention that Aiden's imaginary friend matched the picture found in the library. Nor did I say anything about my dreams. "Some people in town ask if I see a ghost," I answered. "I didn't know what they talked about." I let the subject drop since there was no reason to get Mom worked up, not after my conversation with Jackson. I didn't want her to learn about my snooping around or my jaunts to the old slave cabins. She would refuse to let me leave the house. "Okay, fine. Sorry I brought it up."

I hugged her goodnight and headed up to my room, where I immediately got on my laptop. I wanted more than anything to understand why I dreamed about people and events I had no right to be dreaming about. My dreams had been so vivid that I felt the emotions and stress of the situation.

Truthfully, a small part of me hoped that it was in fact spirits from the other side and not my imagination. It made me sound less crazy to a normal person. It seemed easier to deal with somehow. And with Jackson and Mom both saying I was going too far, I too was starting to wonder if I had the entire wrong idea about Roselynn. *Maybe, somehow, I'm making the whole thing up?*

Alone, I searched online for clues on the house and the past occupants, longing to uncover something helpful.

Turns out 8,000 men from Union and Confederate battalions battled in this area for three days. Roselynn, a house-turned-hospital, was commandeered by the Union as a command center—just as one of the women had told me earlier.

Things were starting to make sense. That's why Lynn Hamilton's house, although located in the South, was home to recuperating Union soldiers. And with her father, General Hamilton, fighting for the Confederates, it makes sense that the house was left vacant. It's likely that the rest of the Hamilton family fled when the battles approached. But why did Lynn stay, and why was she involved in helping soldiers from the opposite side?

My research informed me that although North Carolina joined the Confederacy in 1861, many of the state's occupants were at odds when choosing who to support. Perhaps Lynn was one of them—her loyalties were divided. But with her father serving as a general in the Confederate army, wouldn't she—*shouldn't* she—support her father's army?

North Carolina, although a Confederate state, was deeply divided. Although Roselynn was a Union stronghold, elsewhere in the area, Union soldiers who were captured by Confederates became prisoners of war, and were sent to one of the prisons in South Carolina. Based on the available information, such prisons offered little hope to those inside. Starvation, beatings, and disease killed many who recovered from their wounds.

Despite that North Carolina was a Confederate state, the Union won, which cemented its strong grip. In Union hands, the railroad got supplies to troops, shortening the war. The Union army stockpiled the necessary supplies and the Confederates didn't, making battles a lopsided endeavor. The strategy to starve them out until soldiers surrendered worked.

The war eventually ended.

Falls Creek, while not much today, was once good for something. The transportation of supplies and nursing men back to health saved countless Union lives like Daniel's.

The thing that stuck with me most was Lynn: Despite that her state and father were supporters of the South, in the end she did what she thought was right: She cared for the soldiers, even if they were on the opposing side.

I sat back, my mind awash with questions. It was 10:00 PM—too late to call Tristan. I hoped his reaction tomorrow would be better than Mom's or Jackson's.

# Chapter 11

The next morning, as I helped Mom clean up after breakfast, my mind spun with questions. I waited to ask Tristan about what I learned, but worried that his reaction would be similar to everyone else's.

When Tristan pulled up the driveway, I immediately pounced. "The battle near here during the Civil War, the Internet says seven hundred men died. Where did the bodies go?"

"Hello to you too Sadie," he said, grinning. "What brought this on?"

"I did research last night. What happened to them?" I pressed.

"A cheery question so early in the morning. Some got buried in town. Others, if identifiable and claimed, went home with relatives. Then there's a mass grave near the battlefield for the rest. The class took a field trip once to see reenactments. There's even a famous museum named after it. Why are you asking about this?"

"Mass graves?"

"With so many dead and no identification, something needed to be done with them. No one claimed them, so the town did the right thing." He faced me with a frown. "Mind telling me what's going on?"

His information made sense. The helplessness of wounded soldiers flashed in my mind. I refused to imagine hundreds of men begging for help or worse. Instead, I asked more questions.

"If so many men have died, why does everybody only talk about the ghost of a girl? Everyone says a girl haunts the house. Right? Numerous people claim this. If men died horrible deaths nearby, why is she the only one people talk about?"

"Who says there's only one ghost?" He grinned.

"What? None of your friends said anything about more than one. They only asked about a girl."

"Well, not here. Around the battlefield weird things happen. Tell me what's going on with all this stuff. You're acting odd." Tristan comforted me by putting his arm around my shoulder. "You're freaking me out."

With a deep breath to calm down, I explained my predicament. "People are right—there is a ghost. Aiden's seen her. In my dreams, the same girl shows up."

"In your dreams? Explain what's going on so I can help you." He sat on the porch and patted the space next to him.

"My dreams involve Civil War soldiers, and a girl named Lynn Hamilton, who used to live here." After I gave him a rundown of my experiences, I waited for Tristan's laughter.

"How do you know her name?" he asked, serious.

"A picture of the house is displayed in the library. It shows the people who lived here during the Civil War. Aiden said she's the same girl who visits him. She's the one from my dreams."

He sat back. "Maybe your subconscious is overactive."

I shook my head and continued. "The other day your friend mentioned someone died in the house. I researched articles about her. Her name was Lynn. She called the man with her Daniel. I found a locket in my room hidden in the floor with the initials *L.H.* With those letters, the necklace must belong to her."

He shrugged noncommittally. "Not much to go on." At least he didn't run for the door. His response, although not as enthusiastic as I would have liked, was better than Jackson's. Thinking about our last conversation at the bookstore made my blood boil.

"So what's your goal here?" Tristan was asking as I came out of my thoughts.

I blinked stupidly. "There's a ghost in my house. I want to figure out what she wants and why she keeps coming to me in my dreams."

He nodded pensively. "First, I'm going to paint the extra bedroom I promised your mom so she doesn't kill me," he said, looking at me sternly. "Even though I want to help you, I have work to do here. We need to first see if there *is* a ghost. You write down what you remember from your dreams and your research. We can go over everything and see if we can figure this ghost out, and what she wants. Sound good?"

I wasn't sure how helpful my list would be, but I did my best. The knowledge of someone willing to listen made me focus easier on the task at hand.

My thoughts were interrupted a short time later when Aiden came looking for a snack. "When does your lady friend visit the most?" I asked him. "Does she come more in the day or at night?"

"At night, 'cause I'm cold so she fixes the covers." He shivered. "She likes when I play with my cars too."

"Does she bother you when she comes?" I asked as I poured him a glass of milk.

"Nope. She's nice. She can tuck you in too." He hugged me, and reached for his glass.

"I bet she would. I'll ask her to." *Or not.* I didn't need to be awakened in the middle of the night with a ghost standing by my bed.

I sent Aiden off to play before checking on Tristan. With plastic-covered floors and furniture, the playroom had an unreal quality. Tristan looked up from painting the baseboards when I walked in.

"Need any help?" I asked.

He pointed and gave instructions. "Put this painters' tape around the frame and the wood grilles."

"If I knew what you were talking about I would help you." I looked blankly in the direction where he pointed.

"The blue tape, grab it."

I did as instructed.

"The window's divided into sections. The grilles are the wood dividers. Put tape around them. I need to paint the wood, not the glass."

I understood. "Okay, I can take it from here."

I reapplied the tape three times before giving up.

"These are filthy. We should replace them with new windows already painted." I held up one dusty fingertip to show Tristan why my suggestion was a good one. He shrugged and turned away, busy.

A few minutes later, I sprayed the glass with window cleaner I retrieved from the kitchen. The last section of the window revealed scratches in the glass. On closer inspection, I saw two small letters purposefully etched into the glass.

"Tristan, come look." I read the marks out loud. "*D.M.*" I paused, thinking whose initials these could be. "Daniel, the man from my dream. He stayed here."

Tristan eyed me. "You never saw this before?"

"No. But these are his. I saw Daniel at this window once." I refused to be deterred.

"Take a picture of the initials."

"What?"

"If we're going to try to figure everything out, you want proof. Get your camera. We can add the evidence to your list."

With my camera retrieved from my bedroom, I did as suggested. I felt so much relief. Finally, someone was willing to listen and offer help.

Back at the kitchen, I added the discovery of the etched initials to my list with a smile on my face.

# Chapter 12

Lunchtime ground our activities to a halt. Near the kitchen table, Aiden and Tristan stood with grins on their faces. I stopped my note-taking to make a quick lunch of sandwiches, chips, and apples. I sent them off to eat in the living room, in a hurry to return to my work.

Afterward, Tristan cleaned up the room he'd finished painting, but his regular job at the hardware store waited. He gave us a ride into town. With Aiden playing in his car seat in the back, I questioned Tristan about the battlefield.

"Where did the main fighting take place? It can't be far." I had given little thought to events leading up to Daniel's arrival at Roselynn. But with history at my front door, I found the subject interesting.

"The battlefield is now the site of a historic location three miles outside of town called the Asheville Battlefield Museum. I can take you sometime if you want, but there isn't much there now, just markers giving the history of the place with pictures on them."

"We can go one day when Mom's home to watch Aiden."

I also asked about Saturday's plans with the group.

"What do you have in mind?" I asked, curious what a fun night entailed in a small town. I didn't want to spend my Saturday night in the packed diner with everyone else.

"I asked your mother about some of us driving into Asheville. It's only thirty minutes away. We'll make it back in time for your curfew. Gives us lots of things to do. Look on your computer this week to decide what interests you so my friends and I can plan."

"I will. It's going to be fun no matter what we do," I admitted. "I need a change of scenery."

After a hurried wave goodbye, Aiden and I were on the sidewalk ready for some fun.

Mom was extra happy to see us. Today, her boss accommodated the curiosity of a five-year-old boy. As the only dentist for the residence of Falls Creek and two neighboring towns, his multitude of patients kept the office busy. Luckily, we showed up during a midafternoon lull.

We stayed only long enough for a quick tour of the office to see where Mom worked. Then, my brother and I hit the town. "We'll be back in a couple of hours. Meet you back here."

With Aiden's hand in mine, we strolled along the sidewalk. I was glad to be out of the house with free time on my hands. We passed few people running errands, and everyone waved hello. Typical. I didn't know everyone, but all the townspeople were friendly.

We window shopped through lunch. Aiden pointed out all the things he wanted in the shop windows. Four months until Christmas and he was already compiling his list. With his chatter I forgot the worries of dreams and ghosts. Running my hands through his curly hair, I laughed, giving him a kiss. "Love you, little man. You're the best."

"Love you too Sadie," he said. "Can I buy a toy?"

"A small one. You deserve a treat. But not expensive," I reminded him.

"How about this?" He chose a large brown dinosaur.

I looked at the price tag. "Let's find something a little cheaper." I fought to keep the anger out of my heart.

After his toy purchase, we headed to the library. At the photographs, I realized one important component of solving the puzzle of Lynn overlooked: The Hamilton family lived for generations in the house I now occupied. When the three of us first arrived, the house was devoid of any personal belongings. Where did all the normal household items go?

If I could find any of the belongings, I had a chance to find information on Lynn.

\*\*\*

"The house is ancient. Where did all the old pictures and things end up?" I asked Mom as soon as she started the car to head home after work.

"Sold off mostly," she responded.

"What?" I protested. "Why would someone buy old family photographs and things if not related to the people who owned them?"

She shot me a look from the corner of her eye. "Why the sudden interest in family things?"

I thought of a lie quickly that didn't mention the word ghost. "In the bookstore, a book on interior decorating demonstrated a bunch of old photographs displayed on one of the pages. I want to do the wall by the stairs."

"Great idea." She smiled at my suggestion. "Not everything got sold off. I'm sure we can find something in the garage."

I smiled, in a hurry to make it home.

"I'm happy, Sadie, that you're taking an interest in the house."

"Well, if we're going to be stuck here for a while, we should make it pretty. It's starting to feel not so horrible," I admitted.

After dinner, enough light in the summer sky gave time for me to go snooping. The window covered in grime and dirt made everything inside impossible to see. The garage door refused to budge. After four attempts to lift the stupid thing, I gave up, stomping back to the house.

"I can't see inside. And the stupid door won't open!" I shouted in frustration.

"Ask Tristan tomorrow. He might have tools."

# Chapter 13

In front of the garage the next morning, I explained the dilemma to Tristan.

"I tried yesterday. No way I can open it without help."

"Let me use my superpowers to come to the rescue." Tristan's arm muscles flexed in a show of strength. Aiden laughed and the two of them showed off, trying to impress each other.

"Well, between you two strong boys you should be able to open the door." I moved out of the way to give them space. "Be my guest."

Despite serious tugging and pulling, the door refused to budge, causing more laughter from the two boys. So much for superhero muscles.

"All your macho talk and you can't either. Can you use tools now?" I grew impatient.

"I didn't bring the right ones for this kind of job. The door's been warped with heat and age." He inspected the frame. "A crowbar won't work. The wood is bad. The door is pushing against the wood frame."

"What do we do? Break the door down?"

"You can't destroy property. It doesn't matter if the property belongs to your family. Let's try another way before we demolish the building." One look at the large crack running down the side of the wall and he laughed. "Or we can push it over."

Tristan walked around and peeked through the side window. "You realize a door is around back. Did you notice?"

Ashamed, I shook my head no, feeling my cheeks flame. But when he tried the back door handle and it refused to budge, I laughed.

"Lucky you. I brought something to fix the lock on this one. The building doesn't have to be blown up to get you in. Let me get it."

With the necessary tools in hand, he tried one final time. After a concentrated effort, a soft click signaled the door would open. Unfortunately, the door still stuck, but Tristan being on the football team had advantages. Strong shoulders provided a forceful shove and the door opened for him.

"Stay here. Flashlights are in the truck. Do *not* go in," he cautioned. "I need to make sure it's safe for you."

When he returned several minutes later with two flashlights, we beamed the light into the darkened room. On one wall was row after row of various tools hung from metal pegs. An oily dusty scent lingered in the air. Three wooden cabinets took up the opposite wall from floor to ceiling. With their hinges broken, the doors barely hung on.

In front of the cabinets, unmarked cardboard boxes remained stacked and covered in plastic.

"Hold on Sadie." Tristan seized my hand. I hadn't even realized I took a step in. "Careful of spiders and things."

"Can we bring a box outside at least?" I asked.

"Hold the flashlight. I'll grab one and set it on the porch for you. Open the box outside, not in the house. Who knows what has crawled inside."

Grabbing the nearest box, Tristan carried it to the front porch.

"Do one at a time," he instructed. "I need to finish the room today. You two gonna be okay?"

With a quick nod of my head, I yanked packing tape off the top of the box.

I gave a silent prayer that no bugs resided in them. When I opened it, I was disappointed: jumbled papers included a phone bill too recent for my purposes. A few more pages extracted from the pile proved more up-to-date than what I needed.

"Aiden, help me take this back to the garage. We'll grab another one."

Inside the damp darkness, I selected one box light enough to carry without help, but before I carried it to the porch, I lifted the lid. Old-fashioned pictures filled a leather-bound photo album. With help from Aiden, the box was soon emptied and a stack of photograph albums covered the entire surface of our kitchen table.

Black and white pictures showed ladies in knee-length dresses, with flowery hats perched on their heads. Well dressed and wearing white gloves, the women reminded me of old-fashioned churchgoers. The men standing beside them wore suits and hats.

Once the protective plastic was removed, I anxiously pulled off one picture to turn it over, afraid of accidentally damaging the piece. I wanted to learn if any information written on the back could prove helpful.

Names and dates were written on the back in faded ink. I would ask Mom if any names matched the relatives who took care of her all those years ago after her parents died.

"Anything interesting?" Tristan peered over my shoulder at the open album on the table.

"I think so. Mostly they're pictures of people who used to live here. Some are from 1910 and some from the '70s. Somebody did a good job of keeping things organized and labeled. I'll take them up to my room. Maybe Mom will recognize some of the people when she gets home from work." I flipped through the rest of the albums searching for any of Mom when she was young, but found none.

On the way upstairs I checked on Aiden, who was content playing with toys and didn't want to be bothered. I continued to my room with the new treasures, happy for something to fill the shelves with.

"Want to go grab another with me? Come on, little man. You need some fresh air," I said, thinking it time for him to get outside. "Which box should we take this time?"

"Pick one, Sadie." He pointed to one toward the back.

The contents were a mess, packed liked someone opened up desk drawers and dumped them into the box with little regard to what those papers contained. I found receipts dating from the 1920s for food and dresses. Pages recording sales of cows, tractors, and wallpaper were jumbled together. This was going to take a while.

I thought about putting the box aside to search a different one. But underneath the papers, I came upon a book that paused my work.

A ledger, filled with neatly formed cursive letters dated from the 1800s, tracked expenses and income from the property. Animal sales, cotton prices, and food receipts covered its pages in neat orderly columns of calculations. The sale and purchase of slaves were meticulously recorded. Their births, deaths, and prices listed in neat straight columns didn't signify the gravity of their existence.

I hurried to show Tristan my discovery.

He flipped through the pages, but his actions didn't mirror my excitement. "This was in one of the boxes? Someone needs to take better care of this stuff."

I nodded in agreement, then directed his attention to what I wanted him to notice. "The book shows the purchase of slaves. Right? That's what it says. I'm not wrong. I saw the slaves in my dreams. They were real."

"True. Everyone in town knows the history of the area. It's not a secret. A number of farms kept slaves around here."

"How did I know about the cabins if not for my dreams? How about slaves?" I reminded him. "I'm not from around here. No one talked about slaves to me."

"Sadie, you live in a place with lots of history. This isn't uncommon," he countered.

"Tristan, before I moved here, I knew almost nothing about the area. I didn't have a reason to care." Exasperated with his irritating logic, I went back to my room to put the book with the others.

At the back window, I pictured cabins the way I saw them in my dreams. The slaves were purchased and sold on this property—I knew that now for a fact. If the slaves existed, so did Lynn and Daniel, right? Tristan wanted tangible proof, and now I had it in my newly discovered ledger.

As my excitement wore off, the realization of how this place operated left me in despair. I couldn't imagine what it would be like to be *owned* by another person. To live or die because a master wished it.

I thought back on my dreams with the workers in the fields, in their long dresses, picking cotton. I couldn't call them workers—they were slaves. How did the family treat them? What happened to them after the war?

People in this area might be knowledgeable about the history of the place, but I wasn't. It would take time for me to get used to the area, what was considered normal here hundreds of years ago.

The odor of roses filled the air as I stood by the window. My heartbeat quickened. I turned around to greet Lynn only to be disappointed to find nothing.

"Lynn, I don't understand how you want me to help you. Point me in the right direction," I said to open air. "Talk to me!"

Silence.

Downstairs, I left the boxes out in the garage and played with Aiden instead. The knowledge that my ancestors owned people and that a dead girl remained trapped on the property weighed heavily on my mind. I'd had enough of this mystery for today.

# Chapter 14

That night, it didn't take long for sleep to come and the dreams to start. Gone were any traces of recovering men in the living room like my previous dreams. The sleeping pallets, bandages, and medical supplies were no longer in view. Evidently, enough time had passed for the men to recover or move elsewhere.

The house, void of people, had a silence that left a heaviness in the air. From the entryway to the kitchen, I heard no one. A stillness about the place I didn't remember from my other dreams followed me as I walked from room to room.

I expected something to happen, as if I were in a scary movie building up to its climax. But I didn't know what to wait for. Never in my dreams had the house been empty or given off a foreboding feeling.

In my dream I walked to what I knew now as Aiden's playroom, to look over the initials etched into the window glass.

When I reached the doorway, a solitary figure in the room startled me. Daniel stood in his officer's uniform, his face tense with a slight frown. He was unhappy. Hands clasped behind his back, he appeared ready to give someone a stern lecture. From my angle, I couldn't see what caused his expression to appear so fierce, but whatever the reason, I was glad not to be on the receiving end of it.

After another moment of silence, I took my opportunity and spoke to him. "I don't understand what's going on. Or how to help you." I didn't think a reply would be given.

"You know what to do. Help her!" He turned toward me. "The answer is right in front of you."

"Stop talking in riddles. What's going on? The two of you are in my dreams all the time." I wanted a point-blank response and was tired of all the secrets.

A loud bang interrupted any more conversation between the two of us, and I was yanked from the dream without further answers. I found myself back in bed.

Only after turning on the lamp did I notice an empty gap in the bookshelf. One ledger no longer stood upright, and instead it lay open on the floor. The bang caused by the book falling woke me up.

I went around the book and navigated downstairs, unwilling to face the chance of having any more unwelcome intruders in my sleep. I slipped by Mom's darkened door on my way down to the kitchen.

Only the hum of the refrigerator broke the stillness in the room. Not even the chirping of insects outside interrupted the night. Everyone and everything slept as I sat alone at the table to gather my thoughts. I crossed my arms on the table and rested my head on them. Nights of irregular sleep were taking their toll on me.

I had a conversation in my head on how to talk to a ghost. A man alive over one hundred years ago sounded crazy. Nothing changed the fact that these people had died.

A soft whisper of my name broke the silence.

"*Sadie.*"

No one greeted me when I looked around the room, my eyes wide and my heart pounding. Instead, an empty kitchen and unwelcome darkness from the other rooms engulfed me.

With a limited amount of courage, I did what so many teenagers in town had done for years: I went to the cemetery. At the back door, I paused mere seconds before heading out into the darkness.

In the yard, I took one look back at the house. The light was still on in the kitchen, but all the other top-floor windows shrouded themselves in darkness. Even my own bedroom window was black…

But the light was on when I left.

I stared at the darkened window.

Flickers of yellow light shimmered in the window. The curtain swayed slightly even though no windows were open to let in a breeze. A gray smoky mist appeared in the space between the curtain and the glass.

The haze swayed back and forth for seconds. But in my shock it lasted forever.

I almost jumped for joy at seeing the ghost everyone talked about. She was not a figment of everyone's imagination!

Excited, yet frightened by what resided in the house, I debated the next course of action. *Do I stay outside in the dark waiting for another appearance, or do I enter the house and confront the thing occupying my room?*

I battled the urge to run back to the house, to blockade the doors and hide under my comforter. No way to lock a door and keep a ghost outside. Not when she was in my room.

Instead, I skipped the trip to the cemetery and returned to the house. I grabbed a blanket from the closet, not brave enough to go upstairs. I left the TV and one kitchen light on so I wouldn't be in the dark alone.

***

Mom found me the next morning asleep on the couch, blanket still on top of me. She shook me awake. "What are you doing down here?"

There was no way to tell her about my adventure out to the cemetery or the ghost sighting in my room, so I rubbed the sleep out of my eyes to give myself a moment to process the night's events. The whole "A ghost came in my room last night so I decided to sleep downstairs" couldn't happen. Not after her refusal to discuss anything supernatural-related. "I couldn't sleep. I watched TV down here for a while. Must have fallen asleep."

Mom bought my lie. "Okay, well I need to leave in a little bit. Get ready to take care of Aiden. Please."

With fingers crossed and hoping not to find anything scary, I arrived at my bedroom door. When I pressed my ear to the door I heard nothing but the typical silence of an unoccupied room.

I took a deep breath, praying to find nothing strange. Hand on the knob, apprehensive to push open the door, I braced my body, not sure what I would find when the door opened.

The view of my room showed an unmade bed, the book back in its place on the shelf, and the light off. The curtained window was still closed. Everything had stayed the same as last night when I left. Nothing had changed or moved.

I hurriedly dressed for the day, unsure of whether to worry about a ghost who stood by the window or to be happy I finally saw her. Despite all the times I asked for her to appear, now I wasn't sure how I'd react if she did. How would I even have a conversation with her?

Either way, for now I wanted out of my room in case she decided to appear again.

# Chapter 15

At Tristan's arrival, I quickly described the events from the night before. I whispered so Aiden wouldn't be scared of my late-night jaunt out back. I didn't want him to tell Mom either.

"Okay, seriously Sadie, calm down. Who goes out in the middle of the night in their pajamas to the cemetery?" He laughed. "Wait, I want to join you."

When he put the words that way, my actions sounded ridiculous. "You and half the town go out there at night. How was I supposed to know she would come? Nothing bad happened."

"After a conversation with some dream soldier guy, you thought it would be a wise plan to go in the middle of the night? Without telling anyone? Are you *serious?*"

I nodded, trying to shove down any feelings of bitterness. *Jackson told me not to meddle in the past. Now Tristan's telling me not to go into the cemetery.*

"Sadie, next time the urge to go ghost hunting hits you, can you call me? I might be able to talk you out of it."

"No, you won't." I shook my head.

"Fine. But if you want to wander around outside late at night, tell me so I know where you are. Better to be safe than sorry. The town's pretty tame, but you live far out. Animals roam out here." Worry filled his voice. "I don't want anything to happen to you."

Unable to argue my choice was not the most rational, I agreed to his request. But I gave no guarantee I would wait for him.

Tristan took off to paint the family room, so I led Aiden outside to the garage, eager to go through more items. I longed for tangible evidence and needed to prove my dreams involved real people who once lived.

Fifteen boxes remained. I set aside those too heavy to move or filled with current objects and searched for a useful one from the time period I wanted.

Many were packed with more care than others. I didn't slow my progress to figure out why someone bothered to store half the things they did. It was ridiculous to save thirty-year-old receipts, I thought. On another day I would go through them and make a filing system of some sort for the loose papers worth keeping.

One box contained old wooden soldiers perfect for Aiden to play with. While he entertained himself with the soldiers, I returned to the garage to go through more boxes.

Silverware and china filled another box. The silver only needed a quick polish to rid the forks and spoons of tarnish, and the china in protective wrapping was in decent shape.

Inside a small container, I discovered two small articles of clothing wrapped in plastic: a small yellowish christening gown and a baby outfit designed for a boy. The pieces were so fragile and beautiful; it was astonishing they were not damaged over time. To keep them safe, I placed them on a shelf in my room.

Back in the kitchen, I found Tristan staring at my mess.

"Good lord, Sadie. Are you opening every single box today?" He eyed the different things set out.

"Ones I think are important. I'll buy proper containers for them the next time I'm in town. Some of the stuff is upstairs if you want to look. Old baby clothes anyway. And pictures." I paused, looking over the mess. "I'll clean up this afternoon. I want to make one more trip outside to check the last few boxes."

Leaving Aiden and Tristan with a snack and instructions not to touch anything, I headed back to the garage for one final trip for the day.

Moving brown cardboard boxes around, I glimpsed a wooden crate storage trunk, sanded smooth and stained a light color. I ran my hands over it. The wood appeared old with scrapes and scratches on the sides. The latch and an old metal lock prevented a peek inside.

Trying to move the heavy trunk proved impossible for me. I ran to the house to ask Tristan for help. "There's an old steamer trunk I can't budge. Can you please bring it to the house?"

He too failed in his attempt. "I need something to get it off the floor. No way I can pick this up and carry it. I'll have to break the lock since we have no key."

"Okay, sounds good." I moved to find something heavy to smash the lock.

"Sadie, I can't break anything without talking to your mom first," he said. "We've talked about this. Everything belongs to her."

My frustration built, and I struggled to keep my impatience under control.

"Fine, I'll call her. Right now." I turned to head to the house for my phone.

"How about this? Organize the mess inside first. Make room for more stuff. Your mom can look things over when she gets home. If she wants, tomorrow I'll lift the trunk and bring it into the house. You can open it then. I'll bring proper storage containers for you."

"Fine." I didn't keep the pout from my voice.

"Don't go all drama on me. Get permission first. Waiting for one day won't kill you."

*If you say so.* I walked away.

***

First thing I did when Mom got home from work was show her the items rescued from the garage. "Mom, I'll organize the papers after I go through them first. I need some time." I pulled some items from the stack before she fussed about the many piles on her kitchen table. "More are outside. Boxes of them, in fact. I'll figure out some sort of filing system," I promised.

"Tristan called today on his way home. He warned me about the mess." She laughed and added, "You've been a busy girl."

"Things are clean. We can eat in the living room tonight," I pointed out, knowing the kitchen was unusable at the moment.

"Take me out to the garage after dinner. Show me what you want opened," Mom instructed. "I already gave him permission to break the lock."

I couldn't contain my excitement and wrapped my arms around her.

*** 

As soon as sleep came, I dreamt.

Lynn and Daniel managed to find time alone together in the woods behind the house. Never before were they so intimate with each other. Moving so her body pressed against his, Lynn laid her head on his shoulder. Daniel put his arms around her in a protective gesture, pulling her closer.

"Please." Her demeanor was one of distress.

Daniel remained silent but cupped her head in his hands, kissing her.

"You can't go back. I refuse to lose you," Lynn pleaded. "I won't."

I felt sick to my stomach, remembering my dreams of the lifeless bodies that war left behind.

"We have no choice," Daniel said. "I am ordered to go."

Neither spoke for a moment, consumed by their grief over parting.

"Let's promise to make the most of life for the next two weeks," he continued. "Dry your tears. I forbid crying. I'll come back for you."

"I pray the war will end soon," Lynn said. "We can have a life together, Daniel. Promise me."

"I promise."

Pulling away from him, Lynn turned around and walked back to the house.

My dream dissolved as the two figures disappeared. Nothing else took its place.

# Chapter 16

The next morning, the scene of Daniel and Lynn preparing to separate replayed in my mind. The thought of Daniel returning to battle made my stomach queasy. For me, he represented a living, breathing human being. As he had been wounded once and almost died, returning to the danger of war didn't seem fair to him.

The irrational part of me longed to find some way to prevent Daniel's return to the dangers of battle. If he stayed, could he prevent Lynn's death? The rational side of my brain knew such thinking stupid. No one could go back and change the past.

Thoughts of Lynn and Daniel stuck with me hours later, leaving me somber. Aiden's carefree banter and laughter that morning did nothing to elevate my despair. Lynn had feared for the love of her life. I didn't need to be a mind reader to understand her anguish of losing him. It was impossible not to think of the horror and pain if I lost my mom and brother.

While I waited for Tristan to show up, my head repeated a never-ending dialogue about a couple whose life ended. When he arrived, I didn't give him a chance to set up his supplies.

"He's leaving," I said as I pulled him from his truck. "Daniel needs to go back into battle. He reports in two weeks." My emotions didn't help my frame of mind as I explained the circumstances of my dream. "I found out last night," I added as I followed him to the house.

"Sadie, all of this because of dreams? Everything happened over a century ago. How do you plan to change history? He's already been sent to war. What can you do?"

"If I can't prevent any of this, why am I dreaming all these things?" I angrily took my frustration out on him. There was nowhere else for me to direct it. Fix the past, stop a murder from happening, and reunite Lynn and Daniel. These were my lofty goals.

"Maybe you're not supposed to alter anything if it's all a dream?" He tried a different route. "Maybe they want someone to know what took place between them."

"That's a possibility."

"Sadie, you know altering the past is impossible. I did some looking into your problem, though." He gave me a big grin. "I wanted to help you. So I've been reading ghost stories. What, are you surprised?"

"Totally."

"Your ghost isn't a scary one. So you'll be fine, I think. How about you open your trunk and find some lost treasure?"

In my excitement, I had forgotten about inspecting the trunk.

"You aren't going to change the past," he repeated. "But maybe you can find something today to help you to stop obsessing about dead people." Tristan put the box in the corner away from the sofa and TV.

"Thank you," I said, looking at the lock that had been broken. "I want to open this in private though. In case I did all this bothering for no reason."

Tristan and Aiden stood over my shoulder. Self-conscious with two pairs of eyes staring at me, I waited for them to leave. Tristan set off to finish the last of the repairs with Aiden while I knelt at the closed trunk.

With one final prayer, I opened the lid and the odor of roses filled the space around me.

Inside I found a thin sheet of tissue paper, folded neatly in half laid on top, covering everything underneath. Under it, I discovered a wooden pull-out shelf.

A pair of cream-colored gloves made to fit a female hand came first. They were clearly too small for my hand; I didn't try them on. Delicate tiny pearl buttons were sewn on the edge, and I was fearful of tearing the seams if I tried them on.

I continued digging through the trunk to find a flimsy blue lace handkerchief with the initials *L.H.* monogrammed on one corner. Next, I carefully lifted the shelf and placed the compartment on the floor.

A leather-bound book with *Holy Bible* engraved in gold on the front greeted me. On the title page in black ink, flowing cursive letters read, *To Lynn, my beautiful daughter. May you find joy in the journey. Love, Papa.* Packed away for safekeeping who knows how long ago.

On the thin, delicate sheets I saw no other writing. Only a small dried flower pressed between the pages.

Placing the book next to the gloves, I dug deeper into the trunk.

Pages of ivory-colored stationary bundled together with twine came next. I untied the lace bow to see who the folded letters were written for. The first one was dated February 14, 1865, written three months before Lynn died. It and fourteen others were addressed to Daniel. The last one was written only two weeks before her death when Daniel already returned to the fighting.

I paused, not wanting to go further. Lynn's bible, her gloves, her letters. I felt as if I had trespassed in someone's life. Reading the pages would be an intrusion on her privacy. I set them aside to continue digging in the remainder of the trunk.

Tissue paper separated the rest of the layers of odds and ends.

A small fabric purse filled with buttons of all shapes and sizes. A blue ribbon tied in a bow. A full sketch pad of drawings. Flowers, slaves in the field, the tree out back. An older woman. The little boy in my dreams. Soldiers in uniform, all unrecognizable.

A silver hairbrush and matching handheld mirror came next. Strands of long blond hair still attached to the bristles.

The last item at the bottom, a small oval frame containing the picture of a Union soldier in uniform.

Daniel.

The man from my dreams.

Bingo.

# Chapter 17

I ran to Tristan with my discovery. "I was right," I said, breathless. I held the picture out for Tristan. "This is him. The man I told you about. He existed. Believe me now?"

Tristan took the frame, giving it a closer inspection. "I never said I didn't believe you. It's just all the things happening are unusual." He rubbed a smudge off the glass with his thumb. "It is certainly old."

"Yes. Lynn's things are in the trunk. All of the letters are addressed to him." Excitement overtook me, and I spoke quickly. "This picture was at the bottom. These people existed."

"You don't know for sure if this is the man you call Daniel."

I stared at him in surprise. Irritated, I counted to three before finding the right words. "Lynn lived in this house. She wrote letters to Daniel. This is his picture. He looks exactly like the man I dream about with Lynn. How can that be circumstantial?" My tone raised slightly. "How would I know what he looked like? I'm telling you, this is the same man from my dream. What more proof do you need?"

"Not enough scientific proof. I understand you're experiencing weird dreams. They could be because of the stories you listen to." To counter the frown on my face he added, "Hard to believe in something you've never seen before."

"The world doesn't always happen in black and white. My dreams are not because of what I've heard. Daniel existed. So did Lynn. Her letters will tell me something about their relationship. They can prove my dreams are accurate."

"Maybe they can. You're telling me your dreams show you the past. The concept is unbelievable." He shrugged. "You're going to have to give me a little time to get used to the fact."

I took the picture back forcefully. "This helps prove they loved each other. Let me read everything. I will find a way to convince you these two people existed."

"I believe they existed," he replied. "Come on, don't be mad at me. I'm trying to help you. I'm not sure how."

I took a minute to let jumbled thoughts twirl in my head, not wanting to upset one of my few friends by being angry at him. "Give me a little time to see what I find out."

Before any more words passed between us, a loud scream tore through the room. Tristan's eyes grew large, as I'm sure my own did. Our bodies tensed and we turned toward the sound.

A child's scream from the room my little brother played in.

Aiden!

***

Tristan and I raced to him, expecting to find him hurt or injured.

Instead, a fog suspended itself in the doorway of my brother's room. Shrouded in a wispy cloud was the faint image of the one person I wanted to see more than anyone else.

I turned to Tristan to see that his face registered surprise and disbelief. I turned back, facing the familiar shadow.

The transparent figure of Lynn floated straight toward me.

My momentary indecision left her time to cross the distance between us, not stopping when she reached me.

Our bodies collided; ice cold air washed over me. My mind ceased functioning. My body refused to cooperate with my brain's commands. I knew nothing but darkness as I collapsed. Time stopped as everything blinked black.

Suddenly I found myself on the couch, a cool rag on my forehead.

My sweet little brother's voice called out as I sat up. "Sadie." Aiden had his teddy bear in his arms and concern on his face. "Tristan says you fell and hit your head. You get a boo-boo?"

Not wanting to frighten him by asking what happened, I focused on making sure he was fine. "Are you okay, little man? You yelled."

"I saw a mouse. I wanted you to come, but you hurt yourself." He innocently stared at me.

"You screamed because of a mouse? You didn't notice anything else?"

For a little boy who regularly played with a ghost playmate, to scream over something so small seemed odd. His favorite things in life involved creepy, crawly dirty bugs. Mice didn't seem different. I didn't know whether to laugh or cry over the absurdity of the situation.

"Nope. A mouse ran along the wall. He wanted my cars."

Tristan offered a cup of water as I sat up. As I sipped he turned to Aiden. "Little man, why don't you go eat a couple of cookies? Bring one back for your sister after you're done. Bet she'd love one."

"Okay." Giving me a kiss on the cheek, Aiden scampered off, happy for his treat.

As soon as he moved out of earshot I questioned Tristan. "Did you see her? You had to see something."

"You don't suffer from a concussion." He ignored my question while peering into my eyes. "Your eyes appear normal."

I was physically fine. Mentally, I was a little freaked out.

"Here's the deal, Sadie. You stood in the hallway blocking my view. I didn't see much except you passing out."

"Are you sure?"

"We ran down the hall. I stopped when you did so I wouldn't run into you. I felt a blast of cold air and watched you collapse. I caught you before your head hit the ground."

"I saw Lynn. I thought she did something to Aiden. She came toward me. I don't remember anything after."

"There was a cloud, some sort of fog. And I felt a chill." He sat next to me on the couch. "I don't know what's happening. You okay?"

Taking off the damp washcloth from my forehead, I sat up. "It was *her*, Tristan. She was right in front of me. The cloud was her. What else could it be?" The fear of hearing Aiden's scream, only to encounter Lynn, shook me. "I'm fine. I don't understand why Aiden screamed because of a mouse. What was Lynn doing outside of his room? Why'd she come at me like that?"

"Ghosts aren't supposed to be afraid of mice," he said.

"What was she doing?"

"I don't know."

"We've got to explain this to Mom somehow before Aiden does. She won't believe me," I warned Tristan. "I'll tell her Aiden yelled about a mouse. I tripped going to him. The end."

"You sure you want to do that?" He sounded hesitant of my plan. "Why not tell her the truth? She should know you passed out, Sadie."

"She won't believe me if I told her the truth." I tried to stand.

"Careful. I don't need you falling again. Though I don't mind saving damsels in distress. You're welcome, of course."

"Really funny." I headed to the kitchen wanting to end the subject. "I'm getting a cookie. I'm fine. Thanks for your help." I needed answers more than a nursemaid. "Don't tell my mother, okay?"

I searched for my brother to share cookies with him and talk.

"What were you doing when the mouse came?" I questioned carefully.

"I had my cars and soldiers," he said between mouthfuls.

"Was Lynn with you?"

"No. She wanted to watch you. She told me."

The cookie in my hand didn't make it to my mouth. I sat shocked at his words.

*Lynn stood by when I opened the trunk?*

"Did you find more toys?" Aiden changed the subject to more important things.

"No. Only some girl things. Did Lynn say she was okay with me looking in the trunk?" Jackson's warnings of not disturbing the past filled my mind.

"She didn't tell me."

Not probing him further, I changed the subject. "We'll need to tell Mom about the mouse when she gets home."

"Can we name it? How about Bob?"

"Mom isn't going to let us keep a rodent." I kept the fact Mom would make sure all the mice disappeared from our house a secret.

***

Back at the trunk, I returned everything to the way I originally found it. Except for the letters. Those I carried upstairs and placed on the shelf in my room.

Afterward, I found my brother in his room trying to make a mousetrap. "Come on, let's go for a walk."

Leaving Tristan and everything behind, we walked outside to clear my head. Fresh air would do both of us some good. Too much happened today to make sense.

In the peace of the woods, we followed the familiar path we had taken before. Birds chirped in the branches and green trees offered shade from the overbearing sun. The drama taking place in the house seemed out of place in this setting.

I found it easy to forget my problems and focus on searching for whatever little boys looked for in the dirt. Aiden's boundless energy and laughter took my thoughts far away from my ghostly encounter. I didn't want to think about anything but spending time with my brother.

"No, we cannot make an ant colony at the house." When he asked if I could keep ants in my pocket I declined. "Mom would definitely not want ants in the kitchen."

"Can we bring some worms?" he requested. "We have lots of dirt and can get a cup."

"Nope. Let's leave nature here. Keep walking and count how many birds we spot today." I took his hand in mine and led him farther down the path.

We walked for ten minutes, stopping every so often to inspect something that caught Aiden's interest. His fascination with his new surroundings brought laughter and joy to him. I soon found myself laughing along with him.

Before long we came upon the rose bush in full bloom.

"Can we take some flowers home for Mommy?" Aiden touched the petals.

"Be careful or you'll prick your finger on the thorns," I warned. "Next time we'll bring scissors and cut some of the roses. Mom will love them."

Being this close to the rose bush reminded me of Lynn.

"Come on, Aiden. Let's go home and check on Tristan."

# Chapter 18

The letters. I had so many hopes pinned on figuring out why she stayed on the property after her death. *I might be able to help her and Daniel.*

Lynn filled her letters with proclamations of love for Daniel. I took extra care not to wrinkle or tear the folded messages because their age left them old, yellowed, and fragile. The ink, gray from the passage of time, covered entire pages. Lynn.

With her father's certain disproval and her Confederate fiancé's upcoming hostility over a broken engagement, Lynn had faced so much drama in her life; it made my complaining about the move seem petty and immature. Reading the words caused me mixed emotions: relief that I had finally proved the two lovers existed, and sadness in knowing how their story ended.

She loved Daniel above all else. When she fell in love with a Union soldier, Lynn challenged her entire upbringing. She shared her desire to be with Daniel, going against her parents' expectations. She rebelled against her upbringing. With the hope to build a life for herself upon the premise of Daniel's return, she agreed to leave everything behind. She was willing to give up her family to start a new life with Daniel.

Most importantly, among the letters I found an admission she never loved the man she was supposed to marry: Matthew. Her murderer.

The pieces clicked together in my mind. Matthew, overwhelmed with jealousy, anger, and hatred when she fell for another man—a Union soldier, no less—was driven to kill.

As I finished reading the pages I was left emotionally drained. Overwhelmed, I sat in the silence of my room.

Matthew W. Sullivan. Arrested in the death of Lynn Hamilton. He came back and Lynn ended up dead.

Lynn didn't kill herself because she lost Daniel. She was killed because she wanted to be with him.

I wanted to cry. After learning of her deepest thoughts, I felt I had lost a close friend.

It was now more than curiosity about what was happening with my dreams. I wanted to save Daniel and Lynn. Their love story needed a happy ending. I wanted to be the one to bring it to them.

# Chapter 19

It was no surprise that my sleep that night was filled with heartache and sorrow. All night I tossed and turned, unable to find a comfortable position. I suffered a series of dreams depicting the aftermath of Lynn's death and its effect on her loved ones.

I saw Lynn's mother on the couch, Lowell—her surviving child—pressed against her chest. The little boy who once sat with his sister and Daniel out in the woods clung to his mother. His face now so familiar, identifiable from the library and my own dreams. He appeared shrunken and frail in size. Neither he nor his mother was able to fathom how Lynn died so unexpectedly.

Time flashed forward, and I saw the Hamiltons huddled around a fresh grave in the family cemetery. The priest read aloud from a book, though his words offered no comfort to his audience. As the service drew to a close, one by one the family members left, eventually leaving the fresh grave alone in the silence.

I saw Daniel, no longer a soldier in uniform, as he stood at Lynn's grave. He appeared older and more weary in civilian clothes. Years had passed. At the angel statue in the cemetery he knelt. Fresh pink flowers in hand, he mourned alone.

The morning proved a blessing when the dawn appeared. Dark circles under my eyes gave the only outward evidence of my fitful sleep. The nightly images might have vanished from my mind, but the sadness did not.

I wanted to plead with Mom about not feeling well enough to babysit Aiden. I wanted instead to spend the day by myself, within the comfort of my bed. But Mom was busy working, and as a single parent she needed me to do my part to help. I couldn't be selfish. I dressed and headed downstairs for the day.

"You okay?" Mom said when I sat down to eat cereal. "You look tired."

"Just a little headache. Didn't sleep well last night." I didn't bother to explain further. No point in talking about what was going on with someone who didn't believe ghosts existed.

She looked at me, concerned. "I need to leave soon. Will you be all right with Aiden? I can call in and ask for the day off."

"We'll play today in the house." I turned to Aiden, not wanting Mom to ask any more questions. "How long a racetrack can we build?" My words brought a huge smile to his face.

"Can we make it go from my room to the playroom?" He raced to his room to get some track.

"You probably own enough cars. Let's try," I yelled after him. I hoped the activity would take away all of the unwanted images floating in my head.

After I finished my breakfast, I sat with Mom for a minute longer.

"Things going well otherwise?" she asked, still concerned about my appearance. "Maybe you're working too hard on the house and at the bookstore."

I rolled my eyes. Yes, being reminded of Jackson was just what I wanted. But maybe he was right—maybe meddling in the past wasn't such a great idea. I was exhausted. "Yes, I'm fine." To change the subject, I reminded her of my plans for this weekend. "You finish your little chat with Tristan about Friday?"

"I did. He seems nice and polite."

"I think so too," I agreed.

"I called yesterday after work. He's waiting to see what you decide. He needs to make arrangements with his friends."

I pushed the unfinished eggs around on my plate. "Glad you're okay with me going out."

"It's good you're meeting people." She stood to gather her things. "Besides, if you don't behave, I'll call his mother and both of you will be grounded forever." She laughed loudly.

It felt good to laugh together. "Love you, Mom." I stuck my tongue out at her.

\*\*\*

Three days passed slowly as a quiet calmness settled over the house. Aiden didn't bring up his invisible friend. The smell of roses never filled the air.

With no sightings or strange things happening, the house stilled. I might not have understood why everything was at a standstill, but the weirdness proved disconcerting. I even missed my dreams. What would happen next? What was the next chapter in the story?

With my newfound ability to rest, I organized the piles I had previously spread out throughout the house. As for the remaining boxes in the garage, anything not usable I threw out. Others I stored in plastic containers to keep better protected. I didn't find anything else pertaining to Lynn. The task of organizing and cleaning helped take my mind off things.

I waited. Life wouldn't always be this quiet.

# Chapter 20

On Friday, Mom requested to leave work early, giving me plenty of time to get ready for hanging out with new friends without having to babysit Aiden. To keep the night stress free, I chose to wear my favorite pair of jeans and a matching top.

This was *not* a date. This was hanging out with friends. No need to impress anyone. Tristan and I had planned a quick stop at the battlefield before we picked up two of his friends. We would then head to Asheville. Casual dressy best for traipsing through a field where soldiers had died. I saw no reason to take a chance of falling on my face wearing the wrong shoes.

After Mom's embarrassing lecture about curfews, Tristan and I took off.

"You sure you want to tour the battlefield? Not much to see." He pulled us away from the house. "It's better with a guide."

"We won't be long. We pass it on our way." I wanted to pay my respects somehow to Daniel. I wasn't sure when I would get a second chance to be this close.

Tristan laughed. "First real ghost haunting adventure I've ever been on."

"We aren't exactly looking for ghosts. It's sunny outside, not night." After seeing Lynn in my bedroom window, I never wanted to hunt for ghosts at night again. Once was enough.

A short drive to the other side of town and we came to a sign marking the Asheville Civil War Battlefield. Since the adjacent parking lot was almost devoid of cars, we turned onto a dirt road and had the place to ourselves.

Manicured lawns with cannons aimed at an invisible enemy greeted us. I imagined soldiers charging across the empty field toward each other, screaming at the top of their lungs.

The rest of the area was not what I anticipated. The rows of cotton beyond the hills of lawn seemed out of place.

When questioned, Tristan explained the battle occurred on the site of a working family plantation. "The location was used by the Confederates to prevent Yankees from getting to the bigger cities."

The historical society in charge tried to keep the grounds as accurate as possible. Part of the land was still owned by descendants of the original builders.

The first marker detailed Confederate troops retreating from Union forces trying to overtake the area. Overrun by the Union, the Confederate army didn't stand a chance.

Outmanned and outgunned, two options remained: retreat or surrender and be a prisoner.

"It seems that there wasn't much of a choice either way. Run for your life and hide from the enemy, or be thrown in a military jail," I said.

He frowned. "I'm glad it wasn't me having to make that choice."

Farther down the pathway stood a two-story house with green trim. Signs marked that it was a family home that was used as a hospital for wounded troops. As we passed earthworks constructed by both sides, rifle pits, and Union entrenchments, I read the signs cataloging events of the three-day battle. Confederate soldiers tried valiantly to stall Union troops, believing reinforcements would arrive at any time. On the third day, overwhelmed and overtaken, Confederates ended up as prisoners or dead.

On the way back to the car, Tristan pointed out the spot where reenactments happened every year. "People cook meals, set up tents, and relive skirmishes over the weekend. It helps bring needed tourists into town. Doctors dressed in period clothing pretend to care for wounded soldiers. It can get exciting."

"I want to come next time," I said.

For our last stop we visited the cemetery. Stone graves identified the final resting place of the original homeowners and subsequent family members. A mass grave contained seventy-nine bodies of unknown soldiers.

It was in much better shape than the one located on my family's land.

Before we left the grounds, Tristan pointed out locations of supposed ghost sightings. "People see shadows moving among the trees and hear sounds of gunfire in empty fields." He pointed in the direction of the fields. "There's the added bonus of moaning sounds coming from invisible people."

If only I could hear Daniel's version of events, to know what he went through. "Dying men transported in wagons to field hospitals and houses…it must have been horrible," I said. My house, seven miles away, made for a long and painful journey.

After our walking tour, Tristan and I headed to pick up his two friends before heading to Asheville.

"You ready to have some fun now?"

I nodded yes.

To keep the conversation light, I put away thoughts of history and focused on having a good time. It felt good to be away from the confines of the house and I wanted to make the most of my outing. I had spent so much time waiting for Lynn to show up, making me feel on edge, expecting something to happen. Normal was a good thing tonight.

The fact that we lived outside of town, with no friends nearby, with only a frustrating mystery about a ghost to keep me busy, made life lonely. I missed people my own age to hang out with. Tonight would be my chance to remedy that. Tonight's adventure made me a normal teenager.

# Chapter 21

After all the weeks living in the quietness of Falls Creek, Asheville appeared huge. I'd forgotten what normal-size cities were like. Tall buildings, busy intersections, lots of cars, and people filling the streets made the night exciting.

Asheville, which had been settled before the American Revolution, represented itself with stately mansions, as well as antebellum houses that survived the Civil War years. The city also played up its history with walking ghost tours, which were advertised on every street corner. Asheville tried hard to retain a sense of history by maintaining its architectural style. The past, evident in our drive through town as we headed to dinner, made sightseeing interesting. We passed small, manicured parks designed as the focal point of neighborhood blocks. Stone fountains with cascading waterfalls for children to play around added to the charm. Tall, leafy trees with benches underneath offered shady spots away from stifling summer days. I found the whole area enchanting.

Not a drop of trash or graffiti anywhere. No metal bars covered windows, or potholes ruined the streets. Well-maintained cars parked on the side of roads gave no hint of poverty. Mothers pushed babies in strollers. Young children tagged along behind, giving an indication of a family-friendly city. The hustle and fast-paced life of California was not in evidence here.

Tristan and his friends filled the time by pointing out historic spots as we made our way to our final destination.

"This place was once home to signers of the Declaration of Independence and Civil War spies hanged for treason," Tristan informed me.

"After a massive fire destroyed half the city, warehouses on the wharf and four surrounding neighborhoods got rebuilt," Charles, Tristan's closest friend, said from the back seat.

We parked near the waterfront. An updated mix of restaurants and shops redone in the design of the Civil War time period offered numerous choices for entertainment. I gazed out over the water. This was where people, animals, and cargo were once bought, sold, and shipped from the docks. Now, people enjoyed themselves on the riverwalk, redeveloped into a bustling area of updated commerce.

With the late afternoon coming to a close, the duskiness of the sky made the city lights reflecting off tall buildings as a backdrop all the more pretty. The skyline sparkled in the distance. The night would be almost romantic, if I had been on a date. I counted myself lucky to have found some new friends in my new town.

We passed old-fashioned gas lamps on the wooden boardwalk and heard conversations and laughter as patrons pushed through restaurant doors. Once we settled on a place to eat, the three boys were perfect gentlemen, even pulling my chair out for me.

"Figured out what you want to order yet?" Tristan asked me a few minutes later.

"What's the best thing to eat?" I asked.

"Well, knowing you love peanut butter and jelly sandwiches, I recommend that. But they don't serve them." His suggestion made me laugh.

Aiden's only request for lunch each day included the same type of sandwich. He and I finally struck a deal— once a week peanut butter and jelly, but he could eat a cookie each day after lunch on the other days.

"Try the chicken alfredo or the lasagna," Mike, Tristan's quietest friend, suggested. "Either one is usually pretty good."

With orders taken, the four of us fell into a relaxed conversation.

"So what do you think?" Tristan asked.

"Can you be more specific?"

"Falls Creek."

I paused to find the right words without coming off as arrogant or condescending. "I like it here. Things are so different from home. I'm not used to life here yet."

"You don't think of here as home yet?" Mike asked.

"Well, I was born in California, and my friends and everything are there. Here, it's not the same." Back home I always had something to do, someplace to be, people to meet. "The house here is so far away from anything." Nothing to rush off to. No one ever hurried to do anything here.

With no sleepovers, no meeting at the corner coffee shop with friends, my life now was different from my life before. Gone were the late-night phone calls with friends, the crushes on boys in our school, and the secrets my friends shared between us. Still, I hadn't talked to my friends since the night before we left to come here. There was no point.

And here in my new life, which distracted me from the realization that I was friendless here

"Once school starts, join a club," Charles said. "If you take honors classes, you'll never find time for anything but studying. You'll have an excuse to be a loner."

"I'm not a club kind of girl." No, most definitely not. More of a few close friends type of girl, not so much invite half the school over for a party.

"You're not going to be antisocial, are you? You can hang around with us. Wouldn't be a bad thing," said Mike. "We can be the four musketeers."

"I'm not going to be nonsocial. Don't be a dork." The idea of hanging around the three of them at school wasn't a horrible idea, though.

"You'll make lots of friends once school starts. Don't worry," Charles reassured me.

"We can keep you company," Mike agreed. "We can get you in all kinds of trouble."

I laughed. "I don't need any more trouble, thanks." I turned to Tristan. "Thanks for your help around the house. Everything looks good. Mom says you're almost done."

The idea of not seeing him much anymore disappointed me. It was nice to have someone not five years old to talk to, and we got along great. Having him around made the house less lonely.

"I should be able to finish up next week. The heavy duty stuff I'm not able to fix, my uncle will take care of."

"I'm glad everything will be done before summer is over."

After dinner and a short walk along the boardwalk watching the paddle boats make their journey upriver, we piled into the car and headed home to make my curfew. Before Mike and Charles were dropped off, I thanked them for a fun evening. I meant my words too. The change of scenery was what I needed.

"You still having dreams?" Tristan asked when we were alone.

"She loved Daniel. Based on the letters, she planned to marry him. She didn't commit suicide. Her fiancé came back and killed her. I'm one hundred percent sure."

"That's something at least."

"Nothing answers why Daniel asked for help in my dreams, though. How does he want me to save her if she's already dead? He came back when the war ended in my dreams. No one talks about his ghost being around the house. Why would he even be in my dreams?"

"The whole thing is strange. But I know it'll work out," he replied.

In the silence, Tristan reached over and patted my hand. With the night turning chilly as the temperature dropped a few degrees, his touch brought me a sense of comfort.

"Did you have a good time tonight?"

"Yes, your friends are nice. It was fun hanging out with all of you. Thanks for inviting me."

When he pulled into the driveway at home, the porch light was on—Mom's signal to let me know she waited for me.

That's not how the night ended, though. Mom wasn't sitting on the couch pretending to watch TV or read a book. I found her at the kitchen table, gripping a coffee mug with both hands that wouldn't stop shaking.

# Chapter 22

"What's going on?"

Mom sat at the kitchen table, a cup of coffee clutched between her hands. All the downstairs lights were on. I found it hard to believe the time registered 11:00 PM.

Mom's pale face and shaking hands proved disconcerting. The lack of her usual barrage of questions about the evening's activities compounded my confusion.

I stood only a foot away from her. I broke the quiet when I couldn't take it anymore. "You're starting to scare me. Aiden all right?"

A flicker of surprise flashed across her face at the sound of my voice. "I saw a ghost."

These four words weren't anticipated, but explained her behavior.

Mom appeared traumatized but I was glad she experienced something. Now I knew I wasn't crazy, if other people saw ghosts too.

"Where?" Curiosity got the better of me as my tone was excited.

"Out in the backyard. I closed the window for the night." Panic crept into her voice. "A girl looked straight up at me!"

"Her name's Lynn." My words contrasted the anxious tremor in Mom's voice.

"What? How do you know?" She took a deep breath and stared at me with wide eyes.

Sarcastic thoughts tumbled around in my head and fought to escape my mouth, but I paused in order to speak diplomatically. *I've dealt with this for a while now. I talked to you earlier, but you wouldn't listen. In fact, you refused to discuss the topic. Got kind of mad at me, if I recall correctly.*

I didn't actually speak those words. Such a response wouldn't make the situation better.

"She was the daughter of the original owner. The man she was supposed to marry killed her during the Civil War." I skipped over huge sections of the story. No way Mom could handle everything, not in her frame of mind. "I found information at the library about her. She's never hurt anyone. Far as I can tell, she wanders around sometimes."

"You saw her?"

"Yep. So have other people. I tried to ask about her before. Remember?"

She ignored my question. "What are we going to do?"

My mind whirled, trying to come up with an answer. I forced myself to breathe out slowly. Now that Mom had seen her, we could come up with a solution together. We couldn't force Lynn to go away. Ghost exterminators don't exist. The mention of a seance might have sent Mom into hysteria.

"Off to bed. Lynn's never bothered anyone." Better to calm her down now, than have her worked up all night in a panic. "We'll talk tomorrow."

I walked her to the staircase and hugged her goodnight. "A good night's sleep is what you need. Hopefully between the two of us, we can make sense of everything in the morning."

Once I heard the click of her bedroom door, I was alone with my thoughts. Why had Lynn appeared to Mom, now of all times? I went to investigate.

Nothing unusual was visible in the darkness. Lynn left no trace of her presence behind. Finding nothing and heading back inside, I turned off all the lights as I went to my room. I left the silence to itself as I locked up.

In my room, my phone vibrated with an incoming message from Tristan.

*Good night! Thanks for a great time. The guys said they had a good time too. We should do it again.*

I sent him a quick message back.

*Me too. Talk to you tomorrow. Night.*

I didn't tell him about Mom. The morning would be soon enough.

\*\*\*

My night proved peaceful. If I had any dreams, none left a lasting impression on me.

Mom's night, on the other hand, was not restful. In the morning, her frazzled nerves accompanied the shadows under her eyes. It was clear her sleep was interrupted. I chose not to comment about her appearance. Left to my own thoughts, I ate breakfast in silence, waiting for her to bring up Lynn.

"Did you have fun last night, Sadie?" Aiden asked.

"Yes, I did. We'll take you some time to see the big boats on the river."

"Can we ride one?" He looked at Mom for an answer.

"We'll see. I'm not feeling well, Aiden." She focused on her coffee.

"Mommy's tired today. Take it easy on her," I told Aiden.

"Okay." He slipped off his seat. "I like boats though." He headed off to watch TV.

"We'll figure a time to go," I called after him. "Right now I need to get ready for work. You going to be okay?" I directed my question at Mom.

"I don't know. Is it normal to have a ghost in your house?" She brushed the hair out of her eyes, a sure sign that she was nervous.

Sympathetic to her feelings, I hugged her. "We'll be fine, Mom. We can figure this out. We can talk when I get home from work."

I consoled myself with the idea that Mom could help now that she was forced to acknowledge we had a problem.

Best to act normal—since ghost sightings appeared to be a common occurrence, after all.

***

The saving grace at work from the steady stream of people was Tristan dropping in. He took me to lunch at the nearby park, providing a nice distraction. This gave me the perfect opportunity to catch him up with the latest events.

Lunchtime found us under the shade of a tree, sitting on a blanket, sharing food he made and packed himself. Mom's first experience with Lynn ended up taking most of our conversation.

Tristan's response to Mom's plight made me laugh. "I want to see her, not some misty form. It should be my turn," he said with a lopsided grin on his face.

"So you believe she exists now?" I asked.

"Before, I figured it was my friends being stupid. But between what you told me, the fog I saw, and your mom seeing her, it changes things." He flashed a mischievous grin. "The two of you aren't crazy. How fantastic would it be to see her myself?"

"I can't wave a magic wand and make her appear," I said. "She's not a circus animal, following orders."

"Do you think your mom would mind if I spent the night and tried to see her?"

*Yes, she would.* "No way on Earth would she let that happen." I laughed. "Not going to happen. Ever. Come up with something else."

"How about the cemetery? What if I camped out?" he offered as an alternative. "I could record everything just like on TV."

"You realize Mom is freaking out. How does you camping out in the cemetery prove helpful?" I asked. "Besides, you and your friends did enough of that already."

"Why do you think your mom saw her?"

"I don't know." I didn't have an answer after trying to come up with a reason all morning. "You've been out there lots of times. Why haven't you seen her?"

"You make it sound like I live out there. We hang out to tell scary stories and pass the time, not see a ghost."

"You hanging out in the cemetery or sleeping on the couch are bad ideas. Come up with something else." No way did I want to ask Mom either option, though his idea of filming the cemetery wasn't as far-fetched as it sounded.

"We'll come up with something. Who knows, maybe we'll become famous ghost hunters and get rich."

I threw my leftover sandwich at him in response, laughing when it hit him in the face.

In the little time left for lunch, I changed the subject away from ghosts and toward our trip to Asheville. "Thanks for last night. I had a good time."

"We can go again anytime you want." He sounded like he meant it.

"I would love to," I answered. "No cemeteries though."

# Chapter 23

I spent the entire day at work watching the clock waiting for Mom to pick me up and take me home. Her color, not much improved from when she dropped me off that morning, concerned me. She was too quiet on the drive back.

Dishes were piled in the sink and the floor wasn't swept. Nothing indicated that Mom had straightened up the house—not like her at all. I took better care of things when I babysat Aiden, and I hated housework.

At least her hands didn't shake anymore. I took that as a good sign. My brother seemed his normal cheery self so things might not have gone badly for the two of them.

"Aiden and I stayed in town most of the day." She didn't meet my eyes.

I worked six hours. There was nothing to do in Falls Creek for that length of time.

"I don't want to be here by myself." Mom stared at her shoes. "It was quiet and I wanted fresh air."

*Oh please. The reason you don't want to be here by yourself is Lynn,* I thought.

"All day, I've thought about when I was younger. When I stayed here, my room got cold sometimes at night. I thought I saw something once. My aunt and uncle blamed my imagination," Mom continued. "If there was a ghost in the house, maybe my parents were stuck someplace instead of Heaven. Not something an eight-year-old girl wants to think about after her parents died. I wanted to believe them. I convinced myself it was my imagination."

Understanding better her reluctance to talk about ghosts, I gave her a hug. "There isn't anything to be afraid of. Aiden and I are home every day." I thought about Mom's point of view. "Your parents died in a car accident. Lynn was murdered. There's a big difference. Maybe that's why she's still here."

"I don't care. I don't want her here."

"You can't stay out of the house all the time. Be realistic," I rationalized. "We can help her."

Mom offered no contradiction, remaining silent in the face of logic.

"She's been here for decades, longer than us. Why show concern now?" I failed to hide my annoyance. Her past words about the subject and my hurt feelings caused irritation in place of sympathy. I found it ridiculous she wouldn't stay in the house by herself.

I made her sit at the kitchen table as I prepared dinner, finding it easier to maintain my composure by having something to do with my hands.

"Lynn was murdered by her ex-fiancé when she fell in love with someone else. She's been seen by lots of people. Even Aiden. I tried to tell you." I released all the frustration I'd held in for weeks, and fought to keep my voice calm. "You can't stay out of the house. Aiden's played with an invisible friend for months. She's left clues. We need to sort them out. Don't panic now."

Mom sat silently at the table watching me cut up carrots. When she didn't respond, I continued.

"People loved her. She lived here. It's the reason she's still here, I think. We need to help her move on."

"I think she came to my room," she finally admitted.

"What?" I stopped stirring the noodles at the stove to face her. "What do you mean, she came to your room?"

"I used to think my aunt came in at night to tuck me in. What if it was her and not my aunt? What if Aiden's telling the truth?"

I left the kitchen. "I'll be back." Needing a few minutes to myself, I went upstairs. "Watch the noodles," I yelled back toward the kitchen.

In my bedroom I shut the door and spoke to no one in particular. "Your family's long gone. So is Daniel. You need to move on. Nothing is here for you anymore." I pleaded, "I'm sorry it happened, but I can't do anything about it."

The idea of being stuck in a place with no escape, watching my family grow old and die, sounded horrible. I was in uncharted territory persuading ghosts to move on, though. What was I doing here? I pondered things from

Lynn's perspective. To be trapped without the ability to touch or communicate, seeing the world change, while she stayed the same. Did she understand what happened to her all those years ago or the passage of time since then?

There were so many questions to ask, so much evidence I had collected. If only she was willing to talk.

I couldn't be mad at Mom for not wanting to deal with a ghost, nor could I be upset at Lynn for hanging around after being murdered.

Where was I supposed to start? I wanted Lynn not to be trapped. If I could get her to leave maybe she would find her happily ever after with Daniel.

"Lynn, your family isn't here anymore. They loved you. It's time for you to join them. If you don't, you're stuck here. I don't want that for you."

On my computer I looked up ways to catch a ghost. All kinds of crazy schemes popped up, most of them ridiculous. I refused to fill a metal container with soil taken from a cemetery. Once a ghost went into the box, the living closed the lid and buried it on hallowed church grounds. Another explained how to take a glass jar, put a lit candle in it, and once the ghost was inside, put the lid on. None of the listed options applied to helping a lonely dead girl who'd never hurt anyone.

If I couldn't help, how much longer would she be trapped?

Lynn was imprisoned at the house. Why make her world smaller by sticking her in a jar?

"How about this," I told Tristan a few days later. "While we were in Asheville I saw an advertisement for a ghost tour. I'm not expecting ghostbusters to come in, but maybe one of the people who run the tour can help Lynn."

"You think it'll work?"

Since he didn't laugh and instead took me seriously, I worked up the courage to continue. "There's crazy stuff on the internet. Stuff I don't want any part of. But there might be another way. If people can see ghosts, someone might agree to help Lynn."

"Could be worth a shot. How are you going to go about it?" He sounded intrigued.

"I called the tour company and talked to the owner for advice. The lady on the phone passed my number along to a couple of people who might come out and help."

"What are you going to tell your mom?"

"She's willing to try anything now that she's seen Lynn. She doesn't want to worry about a ghost popping up unexpectedly." I didn't add that Mom slept with a night light on now.

***

A week since Mom's sighting and not a glimpse of Lynn, no mention from Aiden of his invisible friend, no smell of roses.

I experienced the uneasy sensation of being watched, though. Unsure if it was Lynn or an overactive imagination

148

playing tricks, I expected her to appear every time I turned a corner. Unlike Mom, the dark didn't scare me anymore.

We went about our daily lives for the rest of the week. In the process, I came to understand how our family home was passed down through each generation. The photo albums, now organized, identified names to match the faces. Other papers recorded daily life through the years. Through wars, the Depression, and other world events, my family managed to hang on to the house.

A sense of peace filled me for the first time since my dad left us. With this house, I understood my family had a sense of security. Dad leaving had left me feeling abandoned and angry. But our ancestral home offered sanctuary. My little family of three were not homeless; we had a place to belong.

Lowell, once grown and married, became the father of a daughter he named Lynn. She became my grandmother, five times removed. The house stayed in the family through all the years.

I spent my time turning freshly painted walls into a place we could call home. The house belonged to us and made me want to make it our home. I did it for Lynn too.

Not to make up for all she lost. Nothing could make up for that.

But in the hopes she realized someone cared.

\*\*\*

Three days later Mom and I prepared for our visitor's arrival.

"I don't think I can do this," Mom admitted. "I'm terrified."

"Mom, don't worry. I know Lynn. I can do this. I want to do this," I said. "Let me talk to her when she comes."

"I should be the one though, I'm the adult."

"But I've known Lynn longer. Mom, really, I'm not afraid. I need to do this for her."

It had taken three phone calls before I came across someone I felt comfortable with enough to invite to the house. After I explained my ghost problem with Juliet, I looked forward to meeting her.

"Sadie, I'm sorry for not believing you earlier. Or wanting to talk about it," Mom said.

"It's okay, Mom. I understand. It must have been hard for you to think about. Let me do this." I hugged her tightly.

Mom relented, agreeing to take Aiden with her the morning our ghost hunter came.

"Thank you for coming," I said to Juliet. On the phone she seemed the most caring and understanding of our situation. When I asked her to come, she was willing. "Would you like something to eat or drink?" Getting acquainted in the kitchen first, before discussing our ghost problem in detail, seemed the proper thing to do.

"Water is fine," Juliet replied.

"I've never been in this situation before. Not sure what to do."

"First off, relax. After our conversation on the phone, I don't believe you have an angry ghost. Nothing I felt so far worries me. Let me walk around a bit alone. We can talk after."

From the back door, I pointed out the backyard and cemetery before sending her on her way. After watching her walk away I settled on the couch in an attempt to read a book and occupy myself while she did her thing.

Once my guest found her way back inside, Juliet shared little information. "Anything in particular you want me to focus on upstairs?" she asked, one hand on the bannister.

"My room belonged to her," I answered. "I saw her once in the backyard out in the cemetery. I might have seen her in my room once." I directed her to my bedroom.

After what felt like hours, Juliet descended the stairs to join me.

She skipped any small talk and got right to business. "There are four in the area."

"Four? Ghosts? How can we have so many?" I stood in stunned disbelief.

"Two are soldiers. Confederates. From what they communicated, they died from injuries after a battle. One predominately stays out near the front porch. I talked to him. He should be moving on."

"No one mentioned more than one ghost." Astounded at the new information, I felt sick to my stomach.

"Think of some ghosts as no more than a whisper of cold air, a slight breeze blowing by you. Such ones are harmless. The other soldier stays out in the yard. I talked to him too."

"And the third one?"

"A man."

"What?"

"He's out by the tree line. He doesn't enter the house or grounds. He refused to acknowledge me," she admitted.

"I don't understand."

"He knows I see him, but refuses to respond to my questions. I feel his anger. He directs his feelings toward the house."

"Why would Daniel be mad?" My thoughts ran in circles in my head.

"It isn't Daniel. His name is Matthew."

My breath hitched. *Matthew?* Juliet's declaration only compounded my anxiety.

The idea of Matthew near the premises upset me. In my eyes he was a killer. Lynn didn't need to be tormented by him in death.

"How can Matthew be here?" I wavered between confusion and horror. "He didn't die here. You must be mistaken."

"He's here now. It is possible," Juliet assured me. "Sometimes after death people go to the place they are most connected to. If he did murder Lynn here as you said, the land would be a significant place for him to return to."

"What about Lynn?" The idea of her being so close to her murderer left me sick to my stomach. "Why does it have to be Matthew? Where's Daniel?"

"Lynn's here now. By the doorway," said Juliet, in a tone so matter-of-fact she could've been talking about what to make for dinner.

I looked over my shoulder, expecting Lynn. No transparent figure, no mist. Greeted by an empty doorway, I looked back to Juliet for help.

"She's there," she assured me. "Talk to her. She's willing to listen better than the other one."

"What do I say?" Talking to air hadn't worked so far.

"Whatever you want."

Where did I start? Should I be angry or hurt she didn't respond at all when I tried to communicate?

"I'm sorry for what happened." With no response from the empty space in front of me, I waited for Juliet to provide advice.

"She's listening." She gave me a friendly smile.

Feeling inadequate, I continued speaking. "Do you realize Daniel came back for you? He kept his promise." Frustrated, I fought back the urge to yell at everyone involved. Juliet was supposed to get rid of a ghost, not increase the number of them.

Silence. My one-sided conversation was increasingly uncomfortable. "All your family is gone. Everyone you knew is gone. There's no reason to stay."

Again, dead silence. I don't know if I expected a verbal agreement, a screech or a cold blast of air, but what I got was nothing.

"She left," Juliet said, as if disappearing ghosts were an everyday occurrence. I guess in her line of work it was.

"What now?"

Since four ghosts hung around Roselynn instead of one, I had no clue what to do. I wasn't an expert in ghosts, and I expected Juliet to solve my problem. "What am I supposed to do? Does she know that Matthew is nearby?"

"You're going to need to find a way to reach Matthew." She made such an action out to be as easy as putting on socks.

"Can't you do it? Where do I to start? I can't do this myself."

"He's not listening to me. He has no reason to. I hold no importance to him."

"Well, he's not going to listen to me either! I didn't know he was there," I pointed out. "He's not going to want to hear anything I say about this whole mess."

At a standstill with neither of us willing to give an inch, we stood facing each other until Juliet finally spoke. "Lynn trusts you. Find a way to convince her. He should move along too."

"Why can't you help her?"

"Ghosts will only listen to who they want to. Like the two soldiers outside. They wanted and needed someone to acknowledge them and let them know it was safe to move on. Lynn can see and hear me, but she won't listen to me. Matthew, stubborn and angry as he is, only pushes me away."

"You're saying if Lynn leaves, Matthew will follow?" I gave in to the fact that the only person to solve this whole mess was me.

"Probably."

"Show me where you saw Matthew." I crossed my arms. "I can't talk to him if I don't know where he is."

Trepidation, fear, and anger followed me out to the woods. On this sunny day with the baby blue sky above us and the chirping birds greeting us, I looked at the spot where Juliet pointed.

I stood three feet away from "Matthew's spot," feeling foolish once again talking to empty space.

"You did a terrible thing. It's too late to fix it now. There's no reason for you to hang around here. Time to move on. Find the light people always talk about."

Not an ounce of compassion or sympathy in my voice. Just irritation of having to clean up everyone else's mess.

I felt alone in this. Mom couldn't cope with this. Aiden was too young. Tristan wasn't interested. Juliet offered no encouragement to me.

Maybe it was the pent-up anger at my father for abandoning us and leaving us broke, or maybe it was the fact I spent my summer away from friends, but I was done fixing everyone else's mistakes. I yelled at the forest where

Juliet indicated Matthew hid out. "Leave! Leave Lynn alone! Leave us alone. You've done enough!"

My imagination played tricks on me, but the leaves on the ground shifted. I didn't have time to be proud of myself for getting rid of a ghost before Juliet spoke, bursting any hope of happiness.

"He's upset, and doesn't want you here anymore." A crisp air blew by us, whipping the hair around our heads and moving leaves.

"So he's still here?"

"You didn't think it was easy, did you?" She laughed.

"It is for you," I told the woman who regularly talked with ghosts as a hobby.

"No. Your two soldiers out front needed reassurance it was safe to leave. They've done their duty and need to move on." She looked at the empty spot where Matthew stood. "Matthew isn't the same. Sometimes they want to stay. Other times they need help to find their way. Once in a while, they cause problems."

"Why would he want to stay near the place he murdered someone?" I asked.

"When people experience anger or fear at the time of death, it can prevent them from moving on."

After informing me of possible options to follow, my guest left with my promises to call her later if anything unusual happened. I didn't point out that our ideas of unusual were different.

A tour of the front yard gave no indication of two soldier ghosts. I didn't know whether to believe Juliet or not. I walked back to the spot Matthew supposedly occupied.

"Sorry for yelling. I'm sure you regret what you did. You need to leave now, though." My voice cracked with emotion. "Please go." My words were likely ignored. I left Matthew to whatever existence he wanted.

I called Mom to come back to the house to pick me up and take us to town. Mom and I sat at the park while Aiden played while I relayed what happened.

"She's nice," I said about Juliet. "She found one soldier on the porch and another in the front yard." Before Mom panicked, I added, "She claims to have sent them away." There was no way to prevent the shock of my next words, though: "Matthew is here. He's in a spot out at the woods."

"Why is he here?" She frowned and chewed her fingernail.

"Juliet wasn't sure. Said he wouldn't listen to her. We're supposed to persuade Lynn to move on and he'll follow."

"She give you any ideas how to do that?"

"Nope." I didn't have the heart to tell Mom we were back to square one with an added ghost on top of it.

"Lucky us." She laughed softly.

***

Later that week, Tristan decided it was time for me to get away from it all and offered to take me somewhere.

"Ask if you can take next Saturday off. You need a change of scenery."

I didn't want to leave the bookstore in the lurch, but I knew he was right. I agreed to call Jackson to cover for me. A whole day without taking care of anyone or anything, or worrying about the past, seemed like heaven. The time away would allow me to clear my head and figure out the next move.

No one knew Matthew was out there until Juliet told us. If he didn't listen to people, he could stay out there.

That philosophy lasted until lunch when Aiden came to tell me that his friend was now mad. We were several feet away in the hallway when I heard sobbing.

"Aiden, what's that?" Hair rose on the back of my neck. I didn't want to walk into the room to find out, but needed to investigate. It was difficult to navigate us down the hallway with Aiden gripping my hand tightly and pulling me closer to his room. I chanced one look at my little brother's face. He didn't appear scared—more like worried as we moved down the hallway.

"Why is she crying?" My mind spun, trying to take it all in.

"She's sad."

"How do you know?"

"She told me."

My thoughts twisted themselves in a knot between helping Lynn and sending my brother safely away.

The sound continued as we stood four feet away from the door, neither one of us moving.

"She wants to talk to you," Aiden said.

*Of course she does.*

He turned, expecting me to make it all better for her. "Are you going to help her?"

"Go get Tristan. He's out in the garage," I instructed my little brother. I needed a moment to myself to figure out what to do. "I'll talk to her," I offered to my brother's retreating back.

When I heard the front door open and close, knowing Aiden was safely away from the crying, I walked the four feet to the doorway, forcing myself to slowly face the room.

Before me stood the almost human-looking form of Lynn. More lifelike than our previous interaction, she was now barely transparent. On a dark night she would have appeared real from a short distance.

Three steps in, the door banged shut behind me and the noise of Lynn's sobbing blasted in my ears full force.

I was paralyzed. Afraid to take my eyes off her. My body tensing.

The ghost walked toward me, tears streaming down her face. Suddenly, silence. Her stillness remained ominous when the crying stopped.

Neither of us spoke as she came closer. Once she stood in front of me I saw how young she was. Two inches shorter than me and smaller in stature, it was hard for me to believe this was the same girl able to care for wounded soldiers and plan a wedding while surviving through a war.

Still, without a sound, Lynn reached out for my hand as if to hold it.

Our worlds emerged as soon as our fingers touched.

# Chapter 24

All her emotions and memories overwhelmed me, pushing out thoughts of my own life.

I found myself in the woods behind the house with Daniel and Lowell, viewing the world through Lynn's eyes. Daniel and Lowell played catch, laughing as the ball dropped between them. In the mere seconds it took for me to understand I was no longer in the hallway, the laughter between them stopped and a figure came out of the woods.

"Matthew, hello!" Lowell didn't realize his friend, with anger on his face and gun in hand, was not a welcome sight.

Matthew slowly advanced toward me, his uniform unkempt and dirty, with a battle-weary expression on his face.

"A Yankee. You left me for a *Yankee*." His words were low and serious.

Daniel whispered to Lowell, and the little boy ran in the direction of the house. With wide eyes, a slight shake of his head persuaded me to remain still. All my instincts shouted to escape, but I refused to leave Daniel defenseless to face Matthew by himself.

"I'm sorry. I love him. Please stop," I—*Lynn*—pleaded as he got closer.

Each of his steps brought the gun closer. Daniel inched his way toward me. One hostile glance at his opponent, and Matthew spoke to me.

"You're mine."

There was little time between hearing the gun go off and the pain in my chest. A searing fire caused me to cry out and tumble to the ground.

In slow motion, Matthew escaped into the cover of the woods as Daniel ran toward me.

As the blood left my body, my heartbeat pounding in my ears, Daniel cradled me in his lap. The red wetness flowed everywhere onto him. His attempts to save my life were useless.

"Love you." I hoped my words reached him.

He kissed me.

The world, a white nothing cloud, surrounded me as a gut-wrenching scream pierced the fog.

I found myself back in the real world, the pain and horror erased. In the short time for Aiden to return with Tristan, I experienced a murder and a lifetime of someone else's memories. I lay alone on the bedroom floor. Lynn was gone, but her memories remained with me.

Lynn had been shot. *I* had been shot. I pulled at my clothes. No blood, no gaping hole appeared on my body. I was left with the residual knowledge of my last memories of Daniel.

Tristan found me curled up in a ball, exhausted from my experience. With his arms around me much like Daniel did for Lynn, Tristan comforted me while I attempted to explain what happened.

"Lynn showed everything. How she died," I stammered. "She touched me and Matthew came out of the woods. He shot her in front of Daniel. *Daniel held her as she died!*"

"I don't know what's going on, but you're okay now. Take deep breaths. I need to see if you're okay."

Still overcome with emotion, I faced Tristan. "I can help Lynn. I become her when she touches me. I can bring her and Daniel together."

"Sadie, what the heck are you talking about? You're not making sense."

"She doesn't realize Daniel is here, as a ghost. For some reason, they can't find each other. We can help them," I tried to convince him this was the only way.

"By letting her invade your body? You sound crazy. Your ghost hunter friend never said Daniel was here. Only Matthew."

"He's here," I pressed. "Give this a chance. We need to try."

"Fine, he's here. But Sadie, you keep passing out every time she gets near you. What happens if she touches you and you fall down the stairs or something? This has to stop. I'm worried about you."

"*We have to do something.*"

He sighed. "How do you suggest we get them together?"

"Lynn touches me. Daniel touches you," I explained simply.

"Really? That's your plan? We let ghosts take over us?" His expression ranged from incredulity to laughter. "Look what happens when she gets close to you."

"It'll only be for a few minutes. Long enough for us to let them see each other and persuade them to move on," I said.

"I don't like your plan."

"Well, do you have any other solutions?"

"No. Still leaves out Matthew though. What are you going to do about him? And what are you going to do about us after we all end up on the ground like you keep doing?"

"Let me work on it. I know I can come up with someone who can help," I assured him.

# Chapter 25

"Jackson, can I talk to you for a minute?" I asked at the bookstore on my day off. "Promise not to be mad."

"I'll try. Depends on what you did." He gave me his full attention.

"Nothing yet. I need your help." I found talking difficult, not sure how he would respond to my request. His last reaction to our conversation about ghosts was in the back of my head. Still, I felt he was the best choice for what I needed done.

With steady nerves, I explained everything that happened since moving to town. Starting with Aiden's first interactions with Lynn, to my dreams and witnessing Lynn's death, to my recent habit of losing consciousness when Lynn touched me. I held nothing back. Honesty was the best option in this situation.

Jackson's face changed from curiosity to hostility and I steeled myself for his reaction. "Is this a joke? Who put you up to this?" The words tumbled out of his mouth, anger evident in his tone.

"What are you talking about? This is no joke. I promise you."

"You have no idea, do you, Sadie? Not a clue." Jackson ran his fingers through his hair.

"What are you talking about?" The direction the conversation headed left me confused.

"My family lost everything when Matthew died!"

This revelation caused me to take a step backward. "Matthew? What does his death have to do with any of this?"

"As the last male heir on the farm, once he died his parents had no one to help to run things. With the scandal of killing Lynn and the effects of the war, they had nothing left." His shoulders collapsed and his anger disappeared.

I still didn't understand his attitude. "And? How does that affect you?"

He looked at me in silence for the obvious to sink into my brain.

"Oh my god, you're related to Matthew."

The possibility never crossed my mind that Matthew and Jackson were related. There was no way for me to know.

Once the truth sank in, I felt ill. He'd been nice to me from the first day we met, and when he offered me a job, and now I was asking him to do something crazy with a dead ancestor accused of killing someone.

"Yep. I'm related to a murderer. Now you understand why I don't hang out waiting for a ghost to appear at your house."

"No one told me. I'm sorry." What was I sorry for, though—because of his family's past or for asking him to be a part of my plan? After witnessing his hurt feelings, I regretted bringing up the entire subject. But knowing this new information helped me proceed with my request. It was too late to take my plea back. I continued.

"People talked about a girl who killed herself and became a ghost when I first moved here. No one ever said anything about you."

"Matthew got caught out in the woods by your house after killing his fiancée. He escaped from jail and made his way back to her house. Shot himself. Her family found the body." He added the last missing pieces to the puzzle. It wasn't something most people realized.

Shocked, I needed time to digest the words.

"With anger at him and us losing the war, the town had a lot to be mad at," Jackson continued. "My family didn't recover. Lost everything. Not something we bring up."

"Why didn't you say anything before?"

"I didn't know you were interested in the subject," he said. "I didn't realize you were still poking around for information."

When my mouth found words again, I said, "How are you related to Matthew?"

"Matthew's younger sister married and gave birth to two children. Until eventually here I am."

"I wouldn't have mentioned any of this. He died near the house?" That explained why Matthew stayed connected to the house. It wasn't only the fact Lynn lived there.

"Most people don't recall all the details. My family does, but we never talk about the past. People only remember what they want to, even if it's wrong. They don't care. Nowadays people only remember a dead girl at your house and that my ancestor killed someone, if they remember anything about it at all."

"That was so long ago. You had nothing to do with any of it. Why would people care about something from so long ago?"

"It's the way things are. What do you want from me?" He took a step backward, putting distance between us.

"Lynn is still in the house. We can help her assist all of them. The only thing is…" I hesitated. I needed his help to do what needed to be done. "I had someone come out to the house. A person who can see ghosts. She saw Lynn and Matthew."

"What? You can't be serious."

"I'm not lying. Please. I need to ask you a favor."

He looked at me, impatient. "Just ask."

"This is going to sound crazy. Please give me a chance to explain." I didn't want him to say no without hearing me out. "I can persuade them to leave if I arrange for them all to be in one location. Lynn shared her memories with me when she touched me. I want to try it with them all. Tristan will do the same with Daniel. I need your help with

Matthew. I didn't know about the two of you. I asked you because you've been a friend and I trust you. If the three of them are all in the same spot, we can persuade them not to be here anymore."

"What's your boyfriend think about this? We aren't exactly best buds."

I laughed. "Tristan's not my boyfriend. He thinks I'm crazy," I admitted.

"There is a chance he's right." Jackson laughed to take the sting from his words.

I smiled back. "He didn't say anything about your history."

"He doesn't know the truth of it probably. Most people don't."

"If it works, think of how great that would be," I reassured him. "Everyone would be at peace."

"I would be crazy myself to let you talk me into this."

"We can do this for them."

At least he stopped frowning when he nodded yes. "Let's give it a try."

# Chapter 26

Three days after my talk with Jackson at the store, the four of us met. Now with the importance of the rosebush understood, it was the ideal location for our undertaking. Juliet, Tristan, Jackson, and I stood there in the forest.

The rosebushes, planted after her death, continued to bloom all these years later. It made sense now—the day I discovered it while on my walk with Aiden. That day when we first moved here and the two of us went exploring seemed so long ago.

Huddled together, our small group faced each other, waiting for Juliet's instructions. We might have been in the middle of summer in the South, but I wore a light jacket, pulling the material around me to stop the chill from seeping in. Whether from the location or nerves because of what we were about to do, my body shivered with cold.

Juliet took control of our nervous little group. "Remember what I told you. Let them come to you. Once they are here, I'll address them. Don't panic if you get scared. Their experiences will become yours. You will feel whatever they do. There is no reason to be frightened by what you see."

"What if they don't want to do this?" Jackson voiced the question we all had but were afraid to ask.

"Keep holding hands," she said, ignoring his question. "I'll do my best to finish this as quickly as possible."

Our small circle with Juliet in the middle made us a strange group of four.

With dusk coming on and the sky beginning to darken, Juliet lit a candle to attract the attention of our invisible friends.

"Matthew, I know you are here. I want to introduce you to Jackson. Your sister gave birth, and their children had children. Jackson is your blood." She gave everyone a moment to gather themselves before she proceeded further. "We're all here to help you. You have no reason to stay away. We mean none of you harm."

The wait didn't cause my thumping heart to return to its normal speed.

"Jackson wants to help you. Please don't shut us out. We can make the situation better for you. Matthew, you were never meant to stay earthbound." Juliet paused to let her words sink in and give Matthew a chance to do what she instructed. "Matthew's willing to join us. He's in front of you, Jackson. Reach out and touch him quickly before he changes his mind."

Jackson reached out blindly for something he couldn't see, his eyes wide. A moment later his muscles tensed, and his grip in mine tightened as his body went rigid.

"Hang on, Jackson. I need to call to Lynn." She turned in my direction. "Sadie, ready?"

At the sound of my name, my body stilled in anticipation. *Don't let me black out like last time before we finish this.* I felt the squeeze of Tristan's hand in mine. The small gesture reassured me I was not alone in this endeavor we all participated in.

"Lynn, he's not here to hurt you anymore. Come into the circle. Give him a chance to make things right."

Nothing happened, making my heart beat all the faster in expectation. I turned toward Jackson, whose eyes were on me, narrowed in anticipation.

"Darn. She's afraid. Sadie, talk to her," Juliet instructed. "Convince her she must come in. We can't finish this without her."

"Lynn, please. Touch me. We're bringing Daniel. But this won't work if we don't do this together. No one can hurt you now. I promise you are safe here."

Lynn's anxiety and sadness transferred to me as she touched my hand. Though I couldn't see her, I instantly felt colder throughout my body. My body moved sluggishly as coldness permeated it while she took over.

Daniel and Tristan came next. This time there was no hesitation as Daniel joined Tristan without prompting.

In our small circle, the dead shadowed over the living. The transparent bodies stood before me, images of Matthew and Daniel blurred over my mortal friends. For a split second, I wondered how I looked through my friends' eyes. We three held hands, staring at each other with eyes wide and amazed.

My body and brain were no longer my own, as Lynn willed my head to turn to her lost love. I let her take over my body without hesitation. I witnessed her thoughts tumbling in my head. The feeling left me with the sensation of floating on air with no control over myself. I tried to relax and let her speak.

"Daniel, I love you." The words felt scratchy coming out of my mouth. Tears streamed down my face, as I felt a profound sadness overtake me. I felt sorrow and regret over what she lost mixed with joy.

"I love you too. I waited a long time. Time for us to be together." Daniel's expression filled with what could only be described as adoration.

Gone was any hint of sternness I witnessed when he addressed me in my dreams. His previous harsh tone was replaced with longing.

The three of us stood, our hands clasped together. But I was afraid one of us would break the circle before we released the souls of the dead.

"Lynn, forgive me. I don't know why I did what I did," Matthew said. "I didn't understand. I only thought of jealousy, how I lost you to a Yankee."

We all waited for Lynn to speak, as uncertainty appeared on Matthew's face. My brain willed my mouth to speak, but nothing came out.

"Matthew, you did a terrible wrong. But time for peace now. Daniel and Lynn are together. They found happiness. Time to leave this place. Time for all of you to leave," Juliet instructed. With her body now facing mine, I saw a hopeful expression on her face. "Lynn, forgive him. No more hate or anger. You all can move on to the next adventure. There is nothing to fear. But you need to help us. Let me help you find peace too."

I mentally willed Lynn to say the right words. I wanted to plead with her to let Matthew go. It was time to release him from his pain and torment.

"Time to move on for everyone," Juliet said.

"I am sorry, Matthew, for not being honest with you. I didn't know how to tell you." Tears slid down my face as I spoke Lynn's words. "I cared about you. I did."

Matthew took a step forward, leaving Jackson's body to face Lynn. Jackson's eyes widened at the separation. As soon as his body was released, a warmness returned to Jackson's hand.

Matthew walked toward the center of the circle, and turned to face me one last time.

"I'm sorry." He disappeared as the candle flickered in Juliet's hand.

Jackson, free at last, let out a moan as his body became completely free of its occupier. To me, his face remained unnaturally pale in the glow of the candle. His hand still in mine, he gave me a tight reassuring squeeze.

"Your turn now. Time to be together," Juliet instructed Lynn and Daniel. "Come here, both of you."

Lynn released my body as she stepped forward. The coldness disappeared, but a tiredness remained. I held firm to my two friends, squeezing their hands to both reassure them and to prevent my body from collapsing on the forest floor.

Afraid words would break the link for Daniel and Lynn, no one spoke.

The two lovers faced each other surrounded by a pale yellow glow. Enclosed by our small protective group, they smiled at each other wordlessly. Their misty presence was so thin that I saw the forest through their bodies. Neither spoke as they moved toward each other, embracing when they were close enough. With one final kiss between them, they slowly vanished in a pale blue light.

A small gust of air blew the flame out, leaving us in darkness as the ground rushed up to reach me and pull me down.

***

"What happened?" I tried to ask, but my words came out as a soft groan. The dirt and leaves underneath me seeped moisture through my jeans.

"Welcome back," Jackson said softly, sitting next to me in the dirt.

"You sure do make a habit of collapsing at the worst times," said Tristan as he sat on the other side of me. "I thought you said you wouldn't do that anymore."

After a moment, I stood with the help of my friends and brushed myself off.

"Sometimes, such an experience makes people tired. You should be okay with some rest," said Juliet. She gave me a hug.

The four of us remained outside in the dark and cold night while I took a moment to gather my strength. After everything I experienced with Lynn, I felt a sadness that I would no longer have her around. This kind-hearted girl whose life was taken away…even in death she cared for others. Being Aiden's *playmate* and tucking him in was proof enough. I wanted one final conversation with her, but now it was too late.

"It's finished." Juliet broke the silence between us and reached for the matches to relight the candle.

"Are they at peace now, do you think?" I needed assurance they were all right. "Even Matthew?"

"In my experience when there is a peaceful ending like what we saw, they will be fine. Everyone went willingly."

"Does this mean you can stop passing out all the time now?" Tristan asked. I laughed in response.

"I hope so."

We returned to Roselynn, the three of us holding hands, as Juliet lit the way with her candle. I smiled knowing I now had two friends who would stand by me no matter what craziness I came up with next.

# Epilogue

At the spot where I witnessed Lynn taking her last mortal breath and where she made a final ghostly appearance, I place a bouquet of white roses every year. I know how much she loved them, so on the anniversary of her death, I walk to the spot and say a silent prayer.

Reunited with their love after over a century apart, whatever Heaven Daniel and Lynn found gave them the happiness they sought for so long.

I hoped Lynn's forgiveness of Matthew gave him peace too. What suffering he experienced on Earth after his death hopefully made up for his mistakes. There was no sign from him, from any of them, since we formed our circle that night in the woods.

Roselynn is mine now. My two children never talk about invisible friends or strange whispers in the dark or having odd dreams. No one complains of being tucked in at night by unknown people. Teenagers no longer show up in the cemetery. Tristan convinced them years ago it was pointless to try to glimpse the mysterious ghost girl.

Someday when my kids are older, I will tell them about their ancestors. I can tell them how a girl fell in love with a soldier boy, and how I helped them reunite over a century later. And if they ask me if I believe in ghosts...I will say yes, I most certainly do.

I knew some.

Made in the USA
Middletown, DE
17 November 2021

52730283R00109